BEAUTIFUL RUIN

ENEMIES #3

PIPER LAWSON

1

RAE

April
Eight months after the fire

*H*ow do you know you've reached the end of a journey?

Is it when the pressure eases enough that you can breathe? When you can sleep through a night without waking up sweaty, questioning the choices that got you there?

I keep waiting for that feeling to kick in. The one that says, "I've made it."

I thought it would happen at Debajo. Or one of the half dozen premiere shows since. Maybe when the top one hundred DJs list came out.

It hasn't.

Now, I'm backstage after playing Wild Fest on a cool night in Colorado.

The Red Rocks Amphitheater is a natural wonder, and I rocked my set.

Sweat rolls down my neck and between my shoulders, joins what's already collected at my low back over the past ninety minutes. My outfit sticks to my body as a circle of guys look over from their booze-filled cups.

"A girl made it to top twenty," one DJ comments as I tug off my wig. "Can't remember that happening."

"You beat Maxx," another says. "Where is that fool?"

"Who the fuck cares?" Eldon, a DJ in his late fifties with wrinkles around his eyes, lifts his cup at me.

I nod in return before going in search of my gear bag backstage. Wig in one hand, I take off my headphones and wind the cord around my hand.

In a dark corner, I bump into someone. "Sorry, I didn't mean to—"

Two guys look up. One has slumped posture and bleached blond hair buzzed short, and the other is Maxx, the DJ I beat out on this year's list.

Maxx tucks something into his pocket and shoves past me, and the other man follows, shooting me side-eye on the way.

I grab my bag, tucking my wig and headphones

inside. My attention lingers on the gems flickering stubbornly in the dark. The diamonds soak up every bit of light, as if they refuse to be ignored.

Not unlike the man who gave them to me.

For the past eight months, I've been to every corner of the globe, but I haven't set foot in Ibiza or seen Harrison King. The man who made a stubborn, suspicious girl fall in love.

The one who took it away because love wasn't as important as his vendetta.

For the first time in my life, I felt what love can do. How it changed me, made me feel alive.

Until it didn't.

I'm not that girl anymore. I have a career I work my ass off for every day, music I love, fans who surprise me... even friends who have my back.

I'm not missing anything.

Say it often enough, you'll start to believe it.

I shut the bag, the tattoo on my wrist flashing.

When I look up again, Maxx has rejoined the circle, settling onto a speaker and pulling a tiny, clear bag from his pocket.

"You think you're the shit?" He sneers. "You aren't until you've played La Mer."

"I don't have anything to prove," I reply evenly.

"Come on. Johnny?" He smirks at the stage manager, who looks away from the act on stage and crosses to the stairs. "You made it if you haven't played La Mer?"

"Fuck no." The guy chuckles before returning to his work.

A hand on my arm has me looking over. It's Eldon.

"Don't listen to him," he chides. "He's jealous."

"Of my tits?" I demand, and Eldon laughs silently. "Because it's not of my career. Asshole makes seven figures a gig."

He shrugs. "After a while, the gigs can blur together. It's the curse of humanity. The price we pay for having the best fucking job in the world—after a while, it starts to feel like a job."

The words reverberate through me. I know what he means.

I glance at Maxx, who's cutting a line of the white powder he bought from the blond guy on the speaker in front of him.

"I was glad to land higher up the list," I admit under my breath. "But how do I even know if I'm better? I stay clean and work my ass off while some of these guys spend more on coke than I do on rent, and they still make a killing."

"You have some good gigs lined up this year."

I'll be performing in LA, New York, London... Plus, I just squeezed in a month at new club in Ibiza called Bliss. "I saved some time for producing."

But I can't kick that thought of La Mer, and Eldon sees the look in my eye.

"If you go chasing after the next club high," he

warns, "you're no different from him."

I shake my head, turning to face the older DJ. "Easy for you to say. You've played La Mer."

His lips twitch. "Once or twice."

I shove a hand through my hair to shake it out after hours beneath the wig. "When we're even, then we'll talk."

Tonight was good, but the high of a job well done is getting shallow and short-lived. Beneath it, I feel empty.

I turn away, but he calls after me. "You ever even visited this Olympus of yours? How do you know La Mer's all that?"

Because I danced under the stars and fell in love with a man who would never stay mine—a man who smelled like the sea and tasted like desperation—and I wanted them both.

"I just know," I murmur.

The man I hated held me as if I was the only thing he needed.

The only thing better was having the man I loved hold me the same way.

But that's over and it's never happening again.

The phone ringing in my hip pocket jars me out of my head.

When I see who it is, I nearly drop the phone.

"Rae." The familiar voice is flat, the British lilt making my gut tighten. "I didn't know who else to call... I need you."

*T*he car pulls up to the London townhouse in the rain.

I took a flight from Denver to New York, then New York to London. Now, I knock on the door, cold from the downpour. The wooden panel creaks open, and I hesitate before stepping inside.

The front hall is narrow, the walls a crisp white with a huge mirror. Facing me is a set of steps leading to the top floor.

Sebastian King sits partway up.

"Nice house." I drop my bag on the floor.

"Bought it last year. Came with almost everything." He shifts back onto his elbows. "Curtains are new," he amends, nodding toward the room around the corner.

I step inside, rounding the wall to see rich, green fabric artfully draped from the high ceilings in the living room around the corner. "Why did you ask how quickly I could get here?"

"Because my season was shit and the year went downhill from there. I have a team awards dinner to attend this evening. And you owe me a date for bailing last year."

I stare him down. *An awards dinner? Are you fucking kidding me?*

Before I can chew him out for dragging me across the ocean, he rises and pads down the stairs to the main floor.

He's pale, his mouth slack and shoulders slumped. He looks as if he's lost weight.

I know what self-destruction looks like. Right now, it wears his face.

"It's been a rough season," he repeats.

But there's humor in his face when he eyes my bag, lifting a brow. "You have a dress in there, or do I need to make you a toga from the curtains?"

Central London is a dense orchestra of pedestrians, buses, cars, and buildings that seem elegant and old enough to have been built into the landscape.

The event is at a venue on Northumberland Avenue, just off Trafalgar Square. When we arrive in a private car, we join the short line as Ash reaches for his phone to show his ID.

If I'd thought it would be hard to find a dress on a few hours' notice in London, I was wrong. Ash gave me the names of a few boutiques.

Before heading out, I couldn't miss the takeout boxes and clothing strewn around the beautiful townhouse.

Between trying on dresses, I did a quick online search to try to find hints as to why Ash looks so strung out. There's nothing, except confirmation in numerous sports publications and blogs that Ash's season was subpar. I guess that much criticism would strain anyone, but that doesn't explain the sudden emergency.

Which means it's up to me to find out.

"You look good in a tux," I inform him as we file into the line waiting to enter.

And he does. Showered and dressed, clad in a custom waistcoat and jacket, Ash is every bit the young, gorgeous athlete.

"Better than Harry?" His grin is almost as quick as usual.

I huff out a breath as the line advances toward the door. "No one looks better in a tux than Harry."

Not that it matters. Harrison's not here, and I can't imagine being in the same place as him again.

I came for Ash, a man I consider a friend. Especially given he called me last year, demanding to know what was going on after Harrison returned to the UK. My explanation was the best one my broken heart could give—we wanted different things.

I wanted him.

He wanted to end Mischa.

Harrison's love for me wasn't enough to overcome his desire for retribution.

It hurt like fuck. Still does some nights, when I'm lying awake and close my eyes and reach across the sheets as if I'll feel his body next to me.

Since then, Ash and I have talked a few times. Texted once a month or so. Now, as the door attendant reviews Ash's credentials and lets us inside, I silently curse Harrison for not keeping tabs on his brother.

Evidently Harrison's too busy for me and for Ash.

In a beautiful, wide hallway, round chandeliers dot the cavernous ceiling. My heels slip into the plush red carpet.

Ash told me in the car that it's a club event in recognition of the staff and players.

With the cocktail reception before dinner, we grab drinks and he introduces me around. But when another player from his club approaches, arm in arm with his stunning girlfriend, Ash tenses next to me.

"Gavin," the man introduces himself to me with an easy smile, but when he claps Ash on the back, the hand lingers.

"Another drink," Ash mutters once they leave.

"You haven't finished that one."

He tosses it back in a single gulp.

I drag Ash into a corner. "Who is he?"

My date shrugs, smirking. "Defender. Not the best one either."

"Strange. You're the one playing defense."

His smile fades.

"Was he giving you shit for a bad season?" I ask.

"On the contrary. He was the only one who didn't." Those blue eyes, so much like Harrison's, streak with self-disgust, and his meaning sinks in.

"Oh. Ohhh." That was why I never saw Ash with a woman last summer. And explains why despite his cheeky charisma, he's private about his personal life. "You were together."

"Shut up, Raegan," he breathes. "Not here."

"Did you break up?" Presumably, given the other guy has a girlfriend and Ash invited me.

"We couldn't break up because, according to him, we never dated. We never did anything."

The words are low and bitter, and I connect the dots. "He's not out." I cock my head. "Are you?"

"Not publicly," Ash concedes. "But that man's so deep in the closet it's a fucking wonder he hasn't emerged in Narnia."

Ash shoots me a wry look before grabbing another drink off a passing tray. A warning goes off in my gut as he drains his champagne, then exchanges it for another.

I grab the full flute from his hand. "Think you're good for now." I square to face him. "Though I don't think it was alcohol that had you sweating when I arrived."

His face falls. "Our season ended, and it was my fault. A play I've made a thousand times before. One I should've made again. I knew it, and they did too. I needed something to numb out."

"So you turned to drugs."

"They turned to me." He grimaces.

"How many times?"

"A couple."

Concern has my hand clenching on his glass. "I'm telling you, it's a bad idea."

A beat. "I know. I'm done with it. I need to figure this out and get back to my life."

"You couldn't call Harrison?"

Before the words are out, I know the answer.

I can only imagine what Harrison would say. Given how their parents died, he'd be pissed if he found out what Ash had gotten into. This was the man who tossed my pills before finding out what they were, who insists on running a clean club in the capital of party drugs.

"He's not perfect, Sebastian."

"But he's strong," he bites out, frowning. "When our parents died. When his fucking building burned, he walked out. Harrison deals with his shit, and even when he does it badly, he does it."

I don't know what to say to that. "All right. Lucky for you, I planned a week's vacation after Red Rock. I'll stick around a few days."

Relief has him sagging. "Thank you."

"But after that, I have business to take care of."

"Stateside?"

I scan the room. "Ibiza."

I need to visit a man I never thought I'd see again. Not one I used to love, but one I used to fear.

Ash's eyebrows lift. He's dying to pry more information from me, but before he can, photographers snap pictures, and we smile and pose.

"This your new girlfriend, Sebastian?" one of them asks eagerly.

The man we spoke to is across the room. His girlfriend's turned to talk to someone else.

Ash leans in to wrap an arm around my waist. "Isn't she lovely?"

I kick him in the calf, and he only bends closer to whisper in my ear, "You've got this down."

It probably looks as if he's murmuring promises in my ear, or a filthy joke.

"Not much to figure out," he adds. "Turn the right angle. Smile the right smile. Pretend you're not secretly hoping they'll drop their camera in the street, where it's run over by a double-decker bus."

I've gotten used to the media this past year as I

climbed a ladder of my own, making it back up to the status I held before the confrontation with Harrison last spring, then I shot right on past it. Wild Fest was only the capstone of an incredible year by any standard. Somehow, my bank account is full enough the bank is sending my own money manager to my rental in LA.

I could buy a condo in any of the cities I frequent, but I haven't yet. Because I'm still adjusting to the new normal—and maybe a little because nowhere I go feels like home.

Flashbulbs go off, and I try to shift away, but Ash slides a hand around to my ass. I'm about to remove it when his words make me stiffen.

"He'd be proud of you."

Tingles start down my spine. As if the man in question is here, even though it's impossible.

I've been avoiding keeping an eye on the tabloids, but I gave in when I hopped on the flight over here. The publications spotted Harrison in New York this week. Regrettably striking in a dark suit and sunglasses. Thankfully alone.

In the image of him crossing at an intersection, phone pressed to his ear, his hair ruffled lightly in the breeze—an inch longer than before, if I had to judge. But the square jaw was the same, the firm lips I've felt on every inch of me, the ones that have whispered comfort and torment in my ears.

I might not be in love with him anymore, but

that doesn't mean I want to see some other woman draped all over him like he hung the sun, and the moon, and the sign at Tiffany's while he was at it.

I look at Ash. "When did you see him last?"

"A few months. While he won't give me details, I suspect he's laying the groundwork to bring Mischa down. As you know, insurance concluded the fire at King's was arson, and there wasn't enough evidence to prove it wasn't Harrison."

My gut twists with guilt. It wasn't my fault, but the fact that the security cameras were off was my doing. All because I wanted to surprise him with the sign.

"Is he happy?" I ask, hating that I want scraps of information about my ex.

Ash sighs. "I've never seen him happy unless he was with you."

Thanks for the gut punch.

Smoothing down my dress, I pretend the words don't affect me. "I'm glad Harrison isn't here now."

Curiosity has him narrowing his eyes at me. "Why's that?"

A knot of tension forms between my shoulders, and I straighten for the cameras. "I need to do something, and he wouldn't want to see me do it."

3

HARRISON

"The robots are suspended from the ceiling to do what—acrobatics?" I demand.

Sawyer leans in, looking impatient. "They serve drinks, you pretentious asshole."

The trendy pub in Brooklyn gave us their prime seating—two low-profile couches and a glass coffee table. Tyler Adams's security is positioned between this section and the rest of the room, dissuading anyone who thinks of coming over or taking a picture.

Mostly, he's watching three grown men have an argument.

"They run on a track"—Sawyer gestures to the space over his head—"along the bar."

"I figured the only club robots were the kind that danced on stage," Tyler comments.

Sawyer shakes his head. "You can use robots for photography, AI for optimizing what's captured. There're clubs in London with interactive walls where you can create your own light displays."

The man across from me is Sawyer Redmond, cofounder of a major tech and industrial company. He's one of a few men I've met who is taller than I am and wearing a Boss jacket and designer jeans like he doesn't give a fuck. His long, unruly hair falls in his face every time he moves, making me itch to grab a fistful and saw it off with a butter knife so I can look him in the damned eyes.

I'm here to see Sawyer about business, but when Tyler said he was in town, I suggested we meet. The only time he had free was now, so I figured I could see two friends at once.

"Sawyer and I went to school together," I inform Tyler. "He was this genius prodigy. Pulling straight As in senior engineering. Hope they kept you warm at night."

"You mean while you used your accent to fuck your way through the female population? You wind up with any souvenirs of that time in your life? I hear chlamydia's a bitch to kick."

"Seems it worked out," Tyler comments, slinging an arm over the back of the velvet couch.

It did, on paper. Sawyer cofounded his company and is on the way to making himself a wealthy man.

I have an empire. One my enemy wants to burn to the ground—starting with Kings last year.

I told myself I could move on and have a future untainted by my past, but Ivanov seems determined to make sure that's not true.

The police weren't able to find the man responsible. I know Mischa was behind it, but I can't prove it.

Since then, his reach has only expanded with new acquisitions fueled by drug money.

I've used the time to regroup.

I will get revenge.

That's the only thing that matters.

Doesn't hurt that you've lost everything else.

A woman comes in the door with a stroller, drawing every eye in the room. She's young and pretty, her red hair tucked up into a bun on her head. She could be a student.

Tyler turns to look over his shoulder as if there's an invisible cord between them.

"He's whipped," he comments as her security guard offers to take the stroller and Annie waves him off. But the second her eyes land on her husband, a smile curving her lips, Tyler's off the couch and at her side.

Sawyer and I exchange a look. "Yeah. It's security who's whipped," he comments. "Figured musicians were supposed to play the field."

Tyler bends to check in the stroller before

straightening, pulling his wife against him for a hard kiss.

"He doesn't. They're in love." I refocus on my friend who's still here, leaving Tyler to fawn over his wife.

"You envy him," Sawyer scoffs.

"Love is an exquisite diversion from the more brutal parts of life."

Last year, I didn't only let myself fall—I practically held the door for both myself and Raegan. At first, I thought I could handle it. Having her at my side felt natural.

Somehow, when I wasn't looking, it switched from natural to necessary. She claimed me, not the other way around. She brought out emotions I'd never felt before, hopes and ambitions I never expected.

After Mischa burned down my property—the future Raegan and I were building together—I vowed I wouldn't let him get away with it. But the farther away I put that in my rearview mirror, the harder it is to remember why I left the woman I love.

I was the one who ended our relationship.

I knew I'd miss her. I didn't expect to lie awake until morning, wishing I knew what ceiling she was staring at.

If she was alone like I was.

If she was *lonely* like I was.

But there's no place for Raegan in my mission.

In the last eight months, I've doubled down on growing my own business, plus invested in having Mischa and his operations surveilled. There's been some sabotage back and forth, me trying to provoke him, but I want it to be done.

What I never told her was that I hoped it would be over soon. That I could find my way back to her when it was done, that I could force my way back into her heart.

It was harsh of me to leave her.

It would have been cruel to promise to return with no guarantee I could.

I force my attention back to the man sitting opposite me. "I'll take three of the bartender robots."

"They're fucking expensive, Harry."

"And I'm fucking rich, Sawyer."

He grins. "Fine. But technology's not your real problem." He shoves his hair back.

Sawyer has a way of seeing straight to the heart of a situation. It comes from his brutal upbringing— while mine was charmed, at least until I was a teenager, his was the opposite. He scraped by.

He'd say he's thriving, and few would argue with his track record and accomplishments. But every victory has a cost—a personal one, if not a public one.

I shake my head. "The prick who was responsible for my parents' deaths."

They might've been ruled overdoses, but it

wasn't their doing. No matter what other ills they were responsible for, they never touched drugs themselves and raised us the same way.

"The police want to nail him for drug trafficking and a raft of other evils, but their timeline feels... infinite," I go on.

Sawyer's eyes darken. "You trust a bunch of paper pushers, you'll be the one bleeding out."

He's speaking from experience. But before I can respond, Tyler and Annie and the stroller approach.

"Congratulations," I say, fixing on a smile.

"Thanks, Harrison." Annie's tight-lipped. "You didn't need to send the stroller, but it's great. It does everything except handle my calendar."

My smirk fades when Tyler says, "Would you like to hold Rose?"

"I don't think—"

Before I can protest, he presses the sleeping bundle into my arms.

Christ. She's all pink and soft, and as her weight settles in my arms, she's not heavy, but precious. She twitches as she wakes, and eyes, dark brown, with little flecks of gold, blink trustingly up at me. Her tiny nose wrinkles, her mouth working. She has a full head of Annie's red hair, and if she has an ounce of her father's talent and her mother's fearlessness, she'll be a force.

She's innocent and loved. I hope it's a long time before she sees the darker sides of the world.

I clear my throat, glancing back up at my friends. "I can see you in her," I tell Tyler.

"Hopefully not for long," he says dryly, tugging his wife against his side as I look back at the baby.

A flash goes off.

"For posterity," Annie says, tucking the phone away as Sawyer and Tyler strike up a conversation.

I'm not sure what she means. "You want a photo of your child with a villain?"

"You're not a villain. Or if you are, she didn't call you one."

Annie holds out her arms. I hand the baby back.

Rae's probably told her I'm a massive prick for how we ended things.

"What did she call me?" I can't help asking.

Annie's gold eyes shine with emotions—a damn rainbow of them. I can see why she's a capable actress. She hitches Rose higher in her arms. "Rae was at an event last night. In London."

It feels like a lifeline. "London? But Wild Fest just happened this past week."

"And you know her schedule."

I'm caught out. "I want to make sure she's safe."

"I was rooting for you guys. Even though it sounds like she's moved on."

With a furtive look toward the stroller, she hands the baby off to Tyler, then retrieves her phone again. She taps the screen a few times before holding it out.

The social media account belongs to my brother's football club, and the date stamp on the post says last night.

The photo on the screen is a kick in the gut.

The woman I love is stunning in a slinky black dress that skims the floor, plunging low between her breasts. She's gorgeous, glamorous, and unlike the Raegan I met a year ago. Her skin glows in the light from the venue and the flashbulbs, her lips full and painted a dark plum. Her dark hair falls in waves around her shoulders, clinging to her perfect breasts.

But it's not her body that makes it impossible to look away.

There's a confidence she wears the fuck out of.

I rip my gaze away from Raegan to take in her companion and get a kick in the gut for my efforts.

Next to her is my brother. His hand rests on her ass and his lips are near her ear, her half smile an afterthought for the cameras given whatever he's telling her.

I clench the phone hard enough my forearm shakes.

This whole time we've been apart, she was still mine from a distance.

Mine when I got off to the memory of her.

Mine when I went to bed questioning whether losing her was worth pursuing the one goal I've had since before I was a man.

She doesn't belong with Ash, not at his side or in his arms.

"Harrison. Are you okay?"

Annie's voice is far away, and I shove the phone back at her.

I'm halfway to the door when Sawyer calls after me, "Where should I send the robots?"

4

HARRISON

"What do you mean he's not in London?" I growl over the phone. "Where is he?"

After the short, tense conversation with one of my staff—whom I'd instructed to drop in on my brother when he wasn't answering his phone—I determine Ash's current location, along with the company he's still keeping four days after the event.

I'm checked out of my Manhattan hotel and on my way to the airport an hour after the close of the business day. The entire chartered flight over, I stew.

When my plane arrives in Ibiza the next morning, I jump in a car, realizing I haven't called Natalia or Toro to let them know I'm coming. An omission that catches me when I barge into my house.

Natalia appears over the upstairs railing. "*Dios mío!* Señor King."

She gets over her surprise and runs down the stairs.

"I'm fine," I assure her.

Her concern turns to scorn. "You didn't call. Toro is out with Barney. I have been working on the gardens."

"I would very much like to see them. Later." My jaw clenches. "I need to find my brother and Raegan. I thought they would be here." I scan my memory for the hotel Ash stayed in last summer. "I'll be back."

Halfway to the door, a voice stops me. "No, señor."

I do a double take because it's the same tone she used to scold me for eating all the salami before my parents' friends could arrive for brunch.

I arch a brow at her glowering face and folded arms. "Toro will be back soon, and he will drive you. In the meantime, I will show you the garden."

"I hope you will be... kind." Toro's gaze meets mine in the rearview mirror.

"I have lots of things to discuss with my brother. None of them are kind."

Like where the hell he got off asking Raegan out, not to mention thinking he could touch her the way he did.

I knew they were friends, but I always figured their common bond was me. I didn't expect them to stay connected without me.

I stare out the window, cracking my knuckles.

"Would you like to hear the news of the island?" Toro asks as he deftly navigates the curving roads.

"Fine."

"Your dog has learned to roll over on command. There is a new hotel in Ibiza Town." He proceeds to regale me, and I half listen until he says, "Ivanov came to the island early for the season."

I straighten. "Why didn't you tell me?"

"You haven't been around."

My teeth grind together. That feels like the damned refrain this week. I'm running a billion-dollar business. I can't be everywhere at once.

"I'm here now," I mutter as the car pulls up outside the hotel. I leap out without waiting for my driver to hold the door.

In the lobby, I tell the concierge, "My brother. Sebastian King."

His eyes widen with fear, and he names the room number. He doesn't want to piss me off.

I jab the button in the elevator, and when the doors open, I stalk down the hallway and bang on the door. Silence greets me.

They're probably out.

Images of them strolling the boardwalks, eating ice cream, and other such nonsense fill my brain.

Or they're inside and the reason they're not answering is that they're otherwise occupied.

I pound on the door again, hard enough it rattles in the frame.

At last, footsteps sound on the other side.

The hairs lift on my neck, and I brace myself for a fight. I'm expecting to see Raegan, but when the door cracks, it's not her.

"Hawhoh, brozuh." Sebastian peers out from the gap in the frame, his mouth full of something, the chain lock still engaged.

"Where is she?" I demand.

"Who?"

I slam a hand against the door, and he jumps.

"Calm down, man."

"Sebastian, if you don't open this door..."

His gaze runs down my form. "You're wrinkled, Harry. You blow in on a tornado?"

I reach through the gap and grab his shirt. "Open. The damn. Door."

Eyes widening, he reaches for the chain and slides it open.

I push the door in and step inside before he can think of getting me back out. My brother looks completely at ease, including the amusement in his expression. He's wearing a T-shirt and boxers, eating...

"What is that?"

"Cinnamon Toast Crunch. Raegan brought it for

me from America." The sound of her name on his lips reminds me why I'm here, why my blood pressure feels dangerously high, before he grabs another bite. "This is good, Harry. They've been holding out on us."

I hit him, hard enough the blow or the surprise sends him to the carpet.

The bowl falls from his hands, and cereal flies everywhere—his face, the carpet, the foyer.

"Jesus," he gasps, rubbing his jaw. "Did you have to do that? Waste a perfectly good bowl of the stuff? This was almost the last—"

"What's going on?"

We both freeze as Raegan emerges from the hall in the suite. She's wrapped in a white towel, her hair dark and dripping around her shoulders.

When she spots me, her mouth falls open. She's obviously stunned to see me, emotions chasing one another across her face. Disbelief. Anger.

"What did you do?" she demands.

It's half her sudden appearance that slams into me and half how she looks.

Fresh, wary, beautiful.

The woman I spent months loving and even longer aching for is here, a few feet away.

"Not nearly enough."

Before I can think twice, I step over my brother and cross the room, grab the back of Raegan's neck, and drag her to me.

I crush her lips beneath mine. She tastes like toothpaste and home, and I kiss her with desperation and anger and exhaustion.

Every trip I've taken, every time I've reminded myself my decision to leave was for the best—it all took a toll on me. From the outside, I might look as powerful as ever. On the inside... my soul corrodes.

I need *her*.

My tongue slips between her lips, stroking and claiming as my fingers tighten in her damp hair. Her scent is floral from her shower, but beneath that, it's all Raegan.

A wet hand grabs my forearm and pushes me away.

My heart hammers as I take in her swollen lips, her hazy eyes.

Of all the decisions I've made in my life, I'd regretted exactly one—telling my parents to get out of the business and causing their deaths.

Since I learned they weren't trying to leave, that regret faded away, replaced with rage and confusion. The past year, I've been angry at them, and at Ivanov for killing them and setting me on a path that made me build a business that would redeem and honor them.

But around the anguish, I've found a new regret: losing this woman.

Because I can't regret loving her, not when the feel of her under me is so jarringly exquisite.

Before I can speak, her palm cracks across my face.

Stars explode behind my eyes, a riot of white and black blossoming as pain radiates up my cheekbone and jaw.

When I can see again, my neck is craned awkwardly and I'm staring at Sebastian reclined on the floor and chewing a piece of rescued cereal.

"Fuck," he declares. "I've never seen a woman hit you before."

But when I turn back to Rae, she looks surprised by her own reaction.

"We need to talk," I say. "In private."

"No."

Frustration rises up. "I'll take you for dinner."

"I have a show tonight."

"It wasn't on your schedule."

I catch my mistake at the same time she does.

"A recent addition," she says.

She's changed since I saw her last. Besides the quiet confidence that's more than skin-deep, she has "recent additions" that come up, independent of me apparently.

Her gaze narrows. "I need to get dressed."

"Need help choosing an outfit?" Sebastian offers from the floor. "The two you talked about on the plane sound good, but I'd like to see them in person."

I could hit him again.

"Both of you stay out," she tells my brother before turning that hot gaze on me again. "If someone so much as knocks on the door while I'm getting ready, I will tear them a new one."

She heads back down the hall, her hips swinging under the towel in a way that has me furious and horny at once.

"If we're done with the violence, you could buy *me* dinner," Sebastian says, grimacing at the mushy cereal pieces on the carpet.

When I came here, I thought I knew my intention—reminding my brother he has no business with this woman. But looking at her, sharing space with her, kissing her...

I know it was a lie. I need Raegan Madani in my life again, and it can't wait until my work is done.

"*N*eed anything?" security half mouths, half yells over the music at my gig.

I shake my head. "No. Why?"

He glances at my setup, and I realize my track's getting stale.

Shit. It happened again. I was staring off into space.

My set at Wild Fest had my full attention, but before that, I caught myself doing this more than usual. Now, thanks to a stop I made earlier today and Harrison showing up at my hotel, my mind is running overtime.

What kind of man barges into your hotel and kisses you?

The same kind who buys and sells clubs like candy.

The kind who drags around a vendetta, who

wears a suit as if it's armor, and when he smirks, panties drop in a ten-mile radius.

I thought it wasn't possible to miss Harrison more than I did these past months, burying it under work and my Little Queen costume. But when he appeared in the living room of the hotel suite Ash rented, rumpled and furious, longing hit me so hard I nearly launched myself at him.

I shoved it down, reminding myself we're on different paths. He's on one he chose over me.

Explicitly.

Remorselessly.

I change the song, segueing into something with a bassline that matches the throbbing in my stomach, and a new wave of energy grips the crowd when they recognize it.

He had no right to kiss me. But from the second his lips crashed down on mine, I was transported to a time and place where I would've done anything for him. For a moment, I forgot everything we aren't, and the friction of his lips and tongue was enough.

If he hadn't pulled back, who knows how long it would've taken for reality to set in?

I shake myself again. I came to Ibiza for work. Both the meeting I secretly took this afternoon, not even letting Ash in on it, and the series of shows I agreed to play at this club for part of the summer.

Harrison King is not part of the plan.

What if he's staying?

A shiver runs through me. I hadn't anticipated that because the reason he wanted to be here—La Mer—is no longer in play. There's no possible explanation for his appearance unless he wants an extended vacation.

As I hit the next transition, a familiar face in back corner of the club has me doing a double take.

Blond hair, buzzed short. A distinctive profile and hunched posture.

It's the guy I saw selling to Maxx at Wild Fest. He's been logging as many air miles as I have.

I watch the club owner approach him, and they argue. The dealer leans in, says something that has the owner pulling back and shaking his head.

Security clearly sees the interaction but doesn't make a move to intervene.

After the show, the owner approaches me. "Thanks for playing. We were lucky to get you at Bliss on short notice."

"Sure. Who needs a vacation?" I flash a smile, but the man only cringes.

"I could use one right about now."

I think about what I saw earlier. "Who was that guy dealing?"

He looks caught out but relents when I raise a brow. "He's one of Mischa's. First showed up six months ago. I should've objected right away, but I didn't until it got worse."

"How bad is 'worse'?" I ask, dreading the answer.

"He's got guys here every night of the week, and rumor has it some of what he was selling was... questionable. I finally put my foot down. Not inside. Not on my property."

"I don't want to look up and see that shit either."

Maybe I'm feeling extra sensitive after seeing Maxx spun out at Wild Fest and after the condition I found Ash in this week.

"Ivanov's started pressuring clubs to sell. Says if they don't, his people will tip off law enforcement that owners like me are allowing this to go down on their watch. I'll lose everything. This way, at least I have money to start over."

"You can't offer to help the police?"

Fear fills his face. "You can't stop this. You'll only be hurt trying."

On my way back to the hotel in the car, I turn it over. Worrying about who controls what drugs in Ibiza is above my pay grade. Except it's in my face every night and it'll only get harder to ignore.

I want a long-ass bath and maybe one of my anxiety pills. But when I open the door to the suite, I know immediately something's wrong.

"Ash?" I step inside, hitting the lights.

Nothing is amiss in the living room. The same stock magazines are on the coffee table.

Except...

I could have sworn I left a sweater on the couch.

There's no way. My stomach knots in disbelief.

I stalk down the hall to Ash's room. His bed is made, his suitcase missing from the stand it occupied since we arrived.

I make my way to my room, my hand shaking as I hit the light.

There's nothing. My belongings are gone.

6

RAE

*T*he fucking nerve.

He did a reverse me. Vanished my belongings.

I place a call on my cell phone to a number I haven't used in a long time.

"Señorita Madani."

"I'm sorry to call so late, Toro. Is he at the villa?"

"I'll come and get you."

"You don't need—"

"I will come."

I remove my wig and finger-comb my hair. There's no change of clothes, so I stalk back downstairs in my same outfit.

The driver arrives, and I shift into the passenger seat, removing the paperback there. My lips twitch when I see the title. *A Gentleman in Moscow*. "How is it?"

"Surprisingly interesting. Thank you for sending it."

"How's your daughter?" I ask.

"I spoke to her this winter." From the hope in his voice, it's progress. "She called on my birthday. After you did."

"You didn't tell Harrison about that?" I caution.

"No." We drive in silence until Toro adds, "We haven't seen him the entire year. When he arrived earlier today, he was distraught."

"I can imagine. He stormed my hotel room like he was laying siege to a castle."

"His anger hides fear."

I shift in my seat, cutting a look across the car. "There was nothing in that hotel suite he was afraid of."

Toro sighs. "Life takes things we do not wish to give. He lost the people he cared about too soon. When his parents passed, he became angry. But it was when he grew quiet that we worried. He is not naturally reserved. Seeing him like that... It is not stable." He cuts me a look.

I cross my arms. "He didn't lose me. He gave me up. There's a difference."

When we pull up at the villa, I shift out and head up the steps to the door. I push on the handle, and it gives.

Inside, memories of last summer ambush me. Making coffee in the kitchen with Harrison. Taking

Barney for his walks. Laughing with Ash on the couch.

There's no sign of any of them, but music comes from somewhere far away.

I head through the villa, the lights on the patio drawing my attention. When I emerge, I see a sight I never thought I'd see.

The brothers are playing soccer barefoot, Ash in a T-shirt and shorts, Harrison shirtless in chinos. Barney is running between them.

What the fuck?

Harrison stops kicking, resting a foot on the ball as he looks between us. Barney attacks the now-still ball, trying to bat it away from Harrison. Until I step onto the patio, my heels clicking on the tile, and the dog lifts his head. His ears perk as he turns toward me.

"Barney..." I hold up a hand of warning, bracing an arm away from my black satin jumpsuit.

With his stunned, deliriously joyful brown eyes on my face, he launches himself at me. I'm knocked on my ass as the creature attacks me with his tongue, seeking any available skin.

"Barney! Dammit!"

It's another ambush, but unlike Harrison's earlier, I can't respond with fists and fury. Instead I wrinkle my nose as I shove at a thick-barreled canine chest and drooling muzzle.

Finally, Ash hooks fingers in the dog's collar and pulls him back.

I shove the hair from my face as I stare up at Harrison. "You kidnapped me," I accuse.

"I kidnapped my brother. Your wardrobe simply came along for the ride." The torch lights play over Harrison's beautiful body, golden hair, and dancing eyes. He's wearing the same smug arrogance as the day I met him, and I'm sorely tempted to tell him where to go as explicitly as I did then.

"Play with us?" Ash calls from where he's dribbling the ball, the dog weaving between his legs in pursuit. "You can even be on Barney's team. He cheats and gets away with it."

I want to hate Harrison. But in this moment, seeing Ash happy and the brothers together and Barney's infectious joy for everything, it's impossible.

Harrison holds out a hand.

"Whatever this is," I warn under my breath, "it stops tonight. I will do more than throw an entire closet of Brioni in the pool. You don't get to fuck with me anymore. We're not together."

An emotion flickers behind his eyes, but it's gone a moment later. He nods.

I brush the dust off my silk pants and take his hand.

7

RAE

"Time for bed," Ash yawns half an hour later.

I drink the beer I've been nursing at the patio table while the guys kicked the ball around, trading stories and jokes.

"What's Barney chewing on?" I ask, realizing the dog has been quiet since knocking me over, content to lie in the corner and ignore both the ball and me.

"Oh bollocks." Ash cringes.

I cross to the dog and pull a pair of panties out of his mouth. "Seriously? You stole my clothes and fed them to Barney?"

"I stole. He fed." Harrison glares at his brother. "Did you not take her bag up to my room like I told you?"

"I thought she'd like to make up her own mind about you."

"Thanks. I think." I frown as I stare at the mangled fabric.

"I'm going to take a shower before bed. Raegan, I'll put your bag upstairs. You two sleep well." Ash disappears into the house, followed by a whining Barney.

It's just Harrison and me.

I drain the last of my beer and grab the other bottles from the table. "When I left, you were ready to beat the crap out of your brother. What changed?"

Harrison waits for me to go ahead of him into the house, and I try to ignore his physicality. He's as strong as ever, naked to the waist, tan, carved muscles. His beautiful eyes track me, his cut jaw twitching.

"I asked him a question. He answered correctly."

Inside, I turn so fast he bumps into me. "Whether I slept with your brother is none of your damn business."

He takes the bottles from my hands and continues toward the kitchen, chuckling under his breath. "That's not what I asked."

The sound of water comes on upstairs. *Ash.*

"What's so funny?" I call after Harrison, not bothering to keep my voice down now that his brother is occupied.

"It's nothing." He deposits the bottles by the sink before returning. "I'm going to clean up here."

I'm surprised, but instead of commenting, I go

upstairs and find my bag in my old room. Unzipping the suitcase, I retrieve my toiletries and some pajamas before realizing Ash is in the second full bathroom.

Harrison's still downstairs, so I head into his bathroom. When I get there, I brush my teeth and wash the makeup off my face. I turn to hang the washcloth on the towel rack, noticing pieces of grass and stuck to the butt of my outfit, plus a smudge that's probably a grass stain from when Barney knocked me over.

This wasn't the plan for tonight. I was supposed to be having a long, hot bath before collapsing into bed at my hotel, twenty feet away from Ash's soft snoring. Instead, I'm in Harrison's bathroom, resisting the impulse to sniff his soap for another hit of familiarity.

I untie the halter neck and strip out of the jumpsuit, tugging it off my bare feet. I'm standing in my underwear, running the fabric under water, when the door opens.

Harrison fills the doorway, a silent, hulking presence. He's stripped down to his shorts, his hard body impossible to ignore.

"Ash was using the other one," I say over the thudding of my heart as I turn back to the sink, continuing to rinse my outfit.

"What is that?" He's at my side the next moment, catching my wrist and turning it over so his thumb presses against the sensitive underside. He traces the shape, and his touch sends my pulse skittering more than the feel of the needle buzzing across my skin.

"A tattoo."

"You copied my scar."

My jaw drops at his audacity. "First, that's not a thing. Second, it looks nothing like your scar. They're crowns. That's the only thing alike. Mine is small. Simple. These parts are curved, and... it's part of my logo. Little Queen is part of me."

I jerk my arm back, balling up the jumpsuit and dropping it on the counter.

Charged blue eyes lift to mine. "Why are you here, Raegan?"

"You're a petulant asshole who stole my clothes."

"In Ibiza."

"You really want to talk about that now?"

"You're standing half-naked in my bathroom," he says softly. "You don't want to know what I want, love."

My eyelids drift down again to the outline of his thick erection against his black shorts.

Distance destroyed my heart, but it fed our chemistry. I've been without him so damn long, and every inch of me is begging to close the space between us. But letting him touch me will mess with my head, make it harder to remember we're not together and we won't be getting back together.

He circles my wrist with his large hand. There's no way he can't feel my thudding pulse.

"Tell me one thing and I'll let you walk out of here. Did you miss me?" he asks.

"No."

His lips caress my wrist, and my knees sag.

"Liar. I can't read your thoughts, but I can read your body. The way your eyes shine. How you breathe through your mouth instead of your nose. The way you sway toward me, daring me to touch you. I know what you want as clearly as I know what I want."

I can't hold in the moan, not when his tongue traces the same path as his lips, sending trails of fire up my arm that have my breasts pulling tight.

His eyes darken with intent. "You have five seconds to leave before I push you against the wall and take what's mine."

"My body doesn't belong to you," I whisper, not moving to leave.

"No. But the way you react to me does. Five."

"You're full of shit."

"You're about to be full of me. Four."

I look past him toward the door. "You'll never have me back, Harrison."

"Three," he rumbles with a wink, and I feel the shiver from that wink all the way through me. "Last chance."

"Go to hell."

"Only if you're coming with me. Two."

I try wiggling out of his grasp, but his grip tightens, pulling my body flush against his. His heat and strength make me gasp.

"Don't play games that I'll win." He swivels around so my back is against the wall. "You knew the second you walked in here where this would end."

Unbelievable.

My heart thuds against my ribs as he waits me out.

I angle up my chin. "Well? Are you ever going to get to one, or is this just—"

He kisses me.

In the quiet moment before his mouth touches mine, I know I could step away, or say no, or even push him away. But I don't. I don't want any of it.

At the first brush of our lips, I open. His tongue slips past mine, and he threads his fingers through my hair, silently begging for more. I give it to him, kissing him back.

His hands drag up my sides, cupping my breasts. The touch feels so damned good, and too soon he's reaching back to unfasten my bra, dragging it down my arms.

He groans against my lips as he grabs my ass. "This get bigger?"

Despite the angst of being apart from him, I've done better at taking care of myself, eating healthy and working out rather than ignoring my body's needs. "This isn't the time to accuse a woman of stress eating—"

"Not what I meant. You're fucking hot, Raegan. Every second that passes, you only get hotter to me."

This is a bad idea. But the arousal pounding through me like a tidal wave won't let me say no.

The apathy I've been dealing with in my gigs, the fatigue, the restlessness, I want him to fix it tonight. And tomorrow can't possibly hurt more than today or yesterday or the hundred days before that.

I brush my fingers across his hard length through the fabric and he twitches against my touch.

I've missed every part of him, including this one. I close my grip around his length, straining to encircle him all the way. A tight exhale forces itself from his lungs, but the look on his face screams approval.

"Yes. Touch me." His hiss turns me to liquid.

I free his cock from his shorts with impatient hands.

He's thick and proud, jutting up toward his clenched abs, his swollen tip already leaking.

My body aches at the sight of him.

"You open that mouth any wider, I'll think you want me to fuck it." Harrison's low rasp strokes along my skin like a dirty caress.

"Keep dreaming."

Far away, I hear the sound of the shower click off.

Harrison boosts me up so I'm braced against the

wall. My breath is uneven, my legs wrapped around his hips and my grip on the back of his neck. Our foreheads press together, his fierce blue eyes boring into mine.

My body's resistance is nothing compared to gravity, and he fills me completely on a single stroke. I'm stretched full of him, our angle making him sink farther into me every time I exhale. The feeling of his cock rooting deep leaves me gasping.

As he rocks into me, I grip the back of his neck, holding on for the ride.

"Jesus, Raegan," he mutters against my ear as if I'm the one tearing him apart instead of the other way around.

When I lean in to kiss Harrison, he fuses our mouths. The kiss deepens, his tongue fucking my mouth while I clench harder around his cock. He shudders, releasing the kiss so I can breathe and cry out.

White-hot pleasure burns, makes me rock my hips against his to chase every bit of friction.

Every second is meant to make up for a day, a week, a month. It has to. Because every gig, every smile, every picture was a lie to bury the truth:

That when Harrison King left me, it took an entire persona to hide my anguish.

He swivels his hips, making me whimper. "You're so fucking tight."

Damn, I'm not going to last. I'm too fucking

sensitive from missing him, and everything about tonight has me wound tighter than a drum. I'm about to go off.

"Come for me," he murmurs.

The next time he pulls back, my back slips down the wall an inch. I dig my nails into his neck. Instinct.

"Not letting you go."

He means he won't drop me. But as the feel of his body, his closeness, his Harrison-ness, drags me over the edge after all this time, and as my orgasm triggers his, making him clench and spurt inside me...

It would be easy to imagine he means something else.

When he carries me to his bed, tucking me in next to him and locking an unyielding arm around me, I could dig an elbow into his gut and run for the door.

I don't.

Tomorrow, things will go back to the way they were, but I let myself have tonight.

8

HARRISON

I've had a lot of filthy fucking dreams.

This one is the best.

Raegan, the woman who's graced every one of my fantasies since the day she ripped me a new one at a friend's wedding, is on her knees. She licks a line up my cock, and my arse clenches as I tug on her hair.

I want her to get serious.

I want her to tease me for goddamned ever.

It's understandable I'd be hard as a bloody teenager the night after I broke down her door, decided to do whatever it took to bring her back to me, only to have her surprise me in my own bathroom. Practically naked. Startlingly beautiful.

The next time we had sex again—I never let myself believe there wouldn't be another time, though during a couple of dark nights, that thought tried to drag me down—I vowed I would be in control. Show her exactly what she's been missing.

But there was no finesse when I took her against the wall. Only raw need, frustration twined around a shriveled black heart that's only ever beat for her.

Now, I'm thinking of all the things we didn't get a chance to do last night.

When I blink my eyes open, the dream gets better.

"Thank fuck," I groan as Raegan comes into focus, her dark hair in sexy tangles around her flushed face. "I was afraid I'd open my eyes and find it was the dog."

"If Barney gives head this good, I'm going to be concerned." Her eyes flash as she rocks back on her heels. The sheet is wrapped around her decadent body, and I want to rip it away.

"Never. You're far better." I shift up on my elbows. "But something isn't right."

"Because I'm naked in your bed?"

"Because it's"—I check the bedside clock—"eight thirty and you're awake."

"I get up early now, asshole."

Those six words hurt.

Because they remind me I've missed out on her life.

She shifts away, and I grab her wrist, tugging her back over me. I press my lips to the tattoo. I hate that she marked herself without my knowing. Without my even knowing she wanted to.

I lace my fingers in hers, pulling her arms down so I can suck one of her nipples. Her back arches, pressing more of her perfect flesh against my mouth as she adjusts her hips across mine. Her wetness glides across my cock, teasing, and I growl.

"Any man who's touched you? I can fuck him out of your head," I promise. "Because I know you in here." I thread my hand in her hair, brushing it back and stroking her temple with my thumb. "And here." I press my other hand to her heart, the steady rhythm thudding beneath my palm.

I'm not angry—I'm determined. Committed.

"I didn't come back for you, Harrison."

Her words land like a blow I wasn't prepared for.

I recover. "For Ash, then."

She shakes her head. "I'm playing La Mer. I went to see Mischa."

Every muscle in my body is tight. Hearing that name on her lips in my bed makes me flip her so fast the sheets get caught between us. "You did *what*?"

"He has a house in Ibiza. I took a meeting with him yesterday before you showed up." She starts to slide out from under me.

No.

I pin her hands next to her head, locking her hips under mine. The expression on her face is irritation, not fear, and that makes me angrier.

How the fuck could she think to just walk in and speak to him?

Everything I've been working toward is a path to ending Ivanov—not to avenge my parents, the way I'd always intended, but to preserve my future. And if I accomplish that, I hope it can be Rae's future too.

Raegan won't have a future if she puts herself in harm's way.

"He's dangerous," I say.

"I understand."

"Clearly you don't. How am I just finding this out now?"

"I should've told you before or after we fucked in the bathroom?" She shifts out of bed and grabs one of my shirts from the closet. "You should probably get dressed. Unless you're hoping Barney will fix that situation for you"—a nod at my cock—"because I'm not going to."

Raegan buttons the shirt and slips out of the room, leaving the door ajar and me speechless.

RAE

"Señorita!" Natalia declares as I come down the stairs, showered and dressed in denim shorts and a flowy black shirt.

"It's so good to see you." I'm not big on gestures, but when the housekeeper hugs me, I can't help returning the squeeze a little.

"Nothing for me?" Ash drawls as he comes down the stairs after me.

Natalia shakes a fist at him. "You made Toro lose money betting on your team."

"You should've bet on the other team," Harrison comments from the kitchen.

"We can't. You're family."

The three of us enter the kitchen, where Harrison is barefoot and drinking an espresso from the machine.

"Lose the French press?" I quip as I get a glass for water.

He stiffens as I brush his hip reaching for the cupboard.

When I mentioned La Mer in bed, he looked at me like a vengeful god ready to rain down fury on hapless mortals. He's clearly not over it.

"On the patio," he bites out before I've had a chance to take a sip. "I don't want Natalia worrying about this."

We head out to the patio overlooking the ocean and take seats on opposite sides of the table.

"Talk."

Though I don't owe him an explanation, Mischa is his nemesis. I understand why he's taken aback.

"I played Wild Fest this year. My career hasn't just recovered. It's exploded," I say. "When the top one hundred list came out, I was swimming in offers. The single I released last fall got new life. I have money."

Sometimes it still feels like a dirty secret.

"I don't own a house, but I could. I could support not only my cousin's charity but half a dozen more."

His jaw works as if he's proud of what I've done but disinclined to deviate from the point he dragged me out here to talk about. "You realize it's not because of the list. It's because of you. You embracing who you are. Playing with joy."

His gaze drops to my wrist, where I'm fingering the tattoo.

It doesn't feel like joy lately. But I don't say that. "I want to play La Mer. That hasn't changed."

The warmth behind his eyes is banked. "Only thing that hasn't."

He rises and crosses to a hedge of bright-pink flowers, pulls off a dead bloom, and tosses it away.

I want to ask why he left the way he did. If it was worth breaking up what we had.

But I'm afraid of the answers. If he says it was worthwhile, it'll hurt all over again.

If he says it wasn't... then what? We can't go backward. I've started to build a future on my own terms, gigs around the world, even if they don't satisfy the way I thought they would.

There's no way I'd give this man a chance to break my heart again. I've done brave things in my life, and stupid ones. Inviting in a man who makes me feel as if I'll never be as worthy as his vendetta would be the most foolish.

"You must have changed too," I say.

"My parents were liars," he says abruptly. "Building a legacy for them is moot."

The hurt in his voice has my chest tightening. "What are you talking about?"

"After Tyler and Annie's housewarming, I received a call from my investigator confirming my parents' life was a lie. They weren't trying to get out, Raegan. If Mischa or his parents killed them, it was to prove a point. For internal justice. Not because they were leaving."

Horror washes over me. I close my fingers around my mug to avoid reaching for him. "You didn't tell me."

"Mischa burned down the club that night. I didn't have a chance."

I can only imagine what he was going through.

He spent his life trying to do penance for what he thought was his fault—that his parents were getting out of the Ivanov's business on account of him and died trying. It must feel as if he never knew them. The anger he must have, the questions... None of which he'll ever get a satisfying answer to.

Fuck. It's not as if this changes everything, but I wish he'd told me.

"So, why continue trying to bury Ivanov?"

Harrison rubs a hand through his hair, looking the kind of rough-around-the-edges he rarely shows the world but shows me because of what we are. What we *were*.

"He's already shaped my past. Not only through his actions, but indirectly, through who I thought my parents were. He's had even more influence than he realizes. I won't let him have my future."

The edge in his voice makes me wonder if he only means his clubs or if that extends to me too. If he was afraid to commit to a future with me so long as Ivanov had a chance of shattering it.

Even if he was, it can't make up for him leaving. But it lets me understand this complicated man a little more, and it makes me want to help.

"He's running drugs through the clubs. Not just his own," I hear myself say. "He's made himself a nuisance at Bliss. And I saw one of his guys at Wild Fest."

Harrison's expression darkens. "Wild Fest... I didn't realize he had territory in America."

"I've seen his people at parties in London." Ash appears in the doorway, hands in his pockets. From his face, I'm guessing he didn't hear the part about his parents.

"You knew it was Mischa's people?" I ask, shoving my hands in my jeans pockets.

He looks away. "Yeah."

"How can you know?" Harrison presses.

"I just fucking do."

Silence falls over us. I think of the coldness in Mischa's eyes before he hit me that night at Debajo. Then last summer, the unforgiving flames devouring every inch of wood, scarring the metal that would have been Kings.

He's the kind of man who would stop at nothing to prove a point.

Harrison pulls out his phone. "Leni. I know you're on holiday. I need you in Ibiza."

There's a response, agitated but not clear enough that I can make out the words.

"I'll make it up to you. Buy you a damn surf school when this is all over." Pause. "Yes, you can get that in writing."

I exchange a look with Ash.

"You've seen what he does. I have to end this." Harrison says it to both of us when he hangs up, but he's looking at me.

I don't answer. Even if he's right and Mischa's evil —the kind of evil that should be extinguished for the benefit of all—his words remind me that I'll never compete with this burning need to see justice done.

"Law enforcement has been monitoring him for a while, but it could still take years to bring him down," Harrison says. "His parents kept their illegitimate operations under wraps being judicious. Mischa is less discreet. But so far, he hasn't slipped up enough to be caught. He rewards loyalty quickly and punishes betrayal even faster."

A shiver runs through me.

"If he's running drugs through clubs beyond his own, outside of Ibiza, we have a hope of catching him. If the management team at Bliss will cooperate," Harrison adds.

I think of how upset the man was. "They're more afraid of Mischa than the law."

He turns to Ash. "What club were you at in London? And why were you even noticing people dealing?"

Ash shifts on his feet, clearly uncomfortable. He doesn't want to admit to his brother what really went down. "I'll tell the police. But I don't want to tell you."

"For fuck's sake—"

"Harrison." I grab his arm, and he turns incredulous blue eyes on me. "I saw a dealer in both places. The club owner confirmed he was Mischa's."

"The man won't flip. Mischa has a stranglehold on this island."

I lean in. "I'm playing again this week. I'll talk to him. And I need to follow up with Mischa."

Harrison seems to draw himself up even taller. "You will do nothing of the sort."

"We'll move back to the hotel today," I say, ignoring him and turning to Ash.

"I'll make the arrangements." Ash grabs his phone and heads to the far side of the patio.

"I will not watch you put yourself in harm's way," Harrison bites out once his brother's out of earshot. He grabs my arm, and I jump more from surprise than his grip.

The sex we had last night doesn't change anything. Not really.

My chin angles up. "Because you're the only one allowed to hurt me?"

His eyes soften as they search mine, and I see the man I fell for. "It's not the same, and you know it."

"No, it's not." The breeze captures my hair and blows it across my face. "Mischa and Zachary never promised to love me before they hurt me."

I take advantage of Harrison's stunned silence to pull out of his hold and head for the door.

9

HARRISON

*M*arina Botafoch is a playground for the rich and one of two docking ports for megayachts.

I wasn't thinking of Raegan when I took one of the cars and came down here after sending her back to her hotel. Now, I'm remembering the time we walked around the harbor together. A year ago, we strolled along this same boardwalk, her asking me questions about the boats.

Weeks later, I chartered her one for one of the best weekends of my life. I'd spend the rest of my life on the damned seas, my stomach rolling with the waves, if it made her smile.

She reappeared in my life yesterday, and she's already leaving it again. I barely got her back, and she's gone.

"Mischa and Zachary never promised to love me before they hurt me."

I hoped in time she'd understand why I left. Now, she sees how dangerous Mischa is... and she still blames me.

I hurt her. But Mischa is capable of ending lives. She must see how much worse that is. How our happiness can't possibly be realized until he's gone.

Regardless, the idea of her being in the same room with the man who's ruined lives and ended others has my gut cold with panic. I can't make decisions from panic.

A young boy playing chase with a friend runs into me, calling out an apology over his shoulder as he continues along his way.

"Harrison." A familiar voice has me turning.

"Christian."

He extends a hand, and I hesitate only a second before taking it.

"Perhaps retirement doesn't agree with you? You look older."

"We all do this year."

"I heard you've been spending most of your time in Paris."

"We are visiting." Christian nods toward a yacht. From this angle, the shiny, white object looks roughly the size of one of Sebastian's football pitches.

"A new prize." I zero in on the name, the *Bijou*.

"Your former jewel has made way for a new one. Looks like the disposal of La Mer was profitable." My words are laced with recrimination.

"In some ways," he says cryptically. "Have a drink with me."

We're not friends or business acquaintances anymore, but given what I learned from Rae, things are escalating with Mischa's business in ways I hadn't anticipated. I'm not ready to turn away possible allies, even if I don't trust them, which is why I asked to meet Christian.

My abs clench as I follow him onto the yacht.

Is this how my brother feels about talking with law enforcement? He acted nervous when I put him in touch with my contact, but he promised to share what he knew. Whatever insights he refuses to share with me.

I'm still angry Sebastian wouldn't tell me—there seems to be a lot of that going around—and that I had to act on good faith. But he didn't give me much choice.

I pull up short when I see the young woman sunbathing.

She rolls over and spots me. "Harrison!" She sits up, pulling a towel across her bare chest.

"Sylvie. I hope you're well."

A man—boy?—lies next to her, frowning protectively.

"I finished university," she says. "Papa said my boyfriend could come on holiday with us."

The man-boy's face relaxes a little at this reinforcement. I hide my smile.

"How nice for you both." With a nod, I follow Christian across the deck.

"He's immature and impulsive and dotes far too much," Christian mutters.

"He's perfect for her."

We take seats at a table at the far end of the yacht, and an attendant immediately brings Christian a cold drink, offering me one as well. I wave him off. From here, we have an uninterrupted view of the sea in one direction and the harbor from the other, white and blue and dotted with color.

"What do you have for me?"

Christian sips his drink. "Advice. I want Mischa gone too."

I arch a brow. "You'll forgive me if I don't trust you."

"What happened last summer was unfortunate. Ivanov threatened Sylvie."

My hands fist under the table. Since LA, I've wondered if that might've been why he changed his mind so quickly about selling La Mer to Mischa.

Christian adds, "At one point in my life, I might have gone toe to toe with him. But I'm too old for a war and too old to risk what I've made on one."

Sylvie's laughter carries on the breeze from the

other end of the boat. Evidently the man-boy is serving his purpose.

"So, it wasn't because of my parents. Who they were."

My host sighs. "No."

I shift out of my chair and cross to the railing. "Then I found out they were liars and criminals for nothing."

After a moment's hesitation, he follows, leaning both elbows on the railing next to me. "Not for nothing, Harrison. You are strong enough to know the truth. To make your own way."

I turn toward him. "I was making my own way."

"You were making theirs. Doing what you thought they wanted, needed. You reinforced that lesson for me when you turned down Sylvie last year. Young people need to find their own way."

I bark out a laugh. "I'm not young."

"Because you never let yourself be. When they died, you took on a challenge they never asked you to."

My next breath is harder than the last despite the fresh air. "I needed to provide for my brother. To prove that I could be the man they hoped."

"You were. They wanted better for you. By choosing to stay away from Mischa's company when they pursued you, you chose the right path. You didn't owe them a single thing after that."

"I need to fight him."

He shakes his head. "If you're going to fight, don't fight for something ugly. Fight for something beautiful."

I think of Kings, a hollowed-out shell. "I don't have anything beautiful to fight for anymore."

"Don't you? How is your lovely American?"

My head snaps around.

"Sylvie pointed out that you two are no longer together. She reads the papers," he explains. "But then, my wife and I had a period of separation. All it accomplished was proving two things: that she was right and I was lonely." His eyes crinkle at the corners.

My fingers flex on the railing. I still don't trust Christian, and having Rae and I publicly linked is a bad idea for her safety.

"She's playing in Ibiza this summer."

Christian nods. "He understands many things, but not love. Keep it from him."

"Then help me end this fast." I can't keep the urgency out of my voice. "I need information."

He hesitates, glancing toward the laughter of his daughter and her boyfriend. "I still have much at stake."

In that moment, I realize the truth. Christian is an old man who likes to talk, to feel important, but when it comes to doing important things, he's a coward.

I shove myself off the railing.

"Where are you going?" Christian calls after me.

"What I know about war is this—most people don't have the luxury of choosing whether they're involved. They can't sell their stake and disappear with their families." I gesture pointedly at the yacht, and he folds his arms.

"I can't help you the way you would like."

I turn my back on him. "Call me when you can."

10

RAE

Of the things that have changed since I got big, one hasn't: Working on a song doesn't get any easier.

Back at the hotel, I'm trying to prepare for my set at Bliss tomorrow night and experiment with new material. I keep reworking the melody, but it doesn't have the vibe I want.

Last year, my tracks were moving towards a more joyful sound—stripped down harmonies, major chords.

Now, it's more minors, but when I'm done, it feels thin rather than atmospheric.

Ash has gone out for a few hours, promising he'll stay out of trouble. But now that he's gone, work is harder because I keep thinking of someone else.

Harrison told me that his parents weren't trying to get out of Mischa's family's business after all.

Harrison spent years deifying his parents only to watch the pedestal he'd put them on crumble. Learning that would fuck up a person. Especially when, that same day, Mischa burned down the club Harrison had spent months building.

He needed somewhere to put that anger, and turning it back on the man who caused all of this probably seemed a reasonable plan.

I wish he'd talked to me instead of leaving.

But it has me thinking that part of why he left was the man who has everything on paper still thinks he doesn't deserve love.

Once, it was because his parents died and he felt responsible somehow. Now, he thinks he's cut from the same cloth as they were.

I wish he could see that they must have loved him. Whatever they did and didn't do, I'm grateful for that.

A text comes through, and I frown at it.

Annie: Has he shown yet?

I hit her contact on my phone, and she answers immediately on FaceTime.

"Hey." Her gold eyes blink, faint circles beneath them hinting at long nights awake.

"Hey. Where's Rose?"

"Uncle Beck's putting her to sleep. He's magic. If I'm lucky, she'll be down for an hour." She moves around her house. "Haley told me to document every moment because Rose will grow up so fast, but I don't know how she found the time."

"Maybe Jax took the pictures."

Annie laughs silently. "Can you picture it? My dad, the paparazzo?"

I shift my notebook computer off my lap and lean forward, thinking back to her text. "How did you know Harrison would be here?"

She tucks a piece of hair behind her head. "Why would you think—"

"Because you're a romantic and you basically outed yourself already," I tell her. "So fess up."

Her nose scrunches. "Fine. Tyler and I saw Harrison in New York a few days ago, and I miii-ight've shared that amazing photo of you and his brother in London."

I huff. "That's why he showed up jealous as hell."

"Did he?" Her lips part, her eyes glazing over dreamily. "I want to know it all."

"You don't have enough testosterone-fueled bull-shit in your life, you're welcome to some of mine."

"Please. Having a three-month-old isn't great for your sex life. Or any life," she admits.

"I could understand if you don't want to have sex."

"It's not me. It's Tyler," she whispers. "He'll stay

up and rock the baby all night. Won't complain once. Then he fell asleep on me last night."

"On you."

"On. Me," she emphasizes.

"Huh." I'm sure it's temporary, because Tyler has seemed one heartbeat away from jumping his wife the entire time I've known them. I fill her in on Harrison's arrival, giving more detail than I normally would.

"He *hit* him and then he *kissed* you?"

"Hit who and kissed who?" A familiar voice comes from out of speaker, and I sigh.

"Hey, Beck."

The screen rotates, and a moment later, they're both in frame.

Beck grins. "Hey, Little Queen."

"Harrison hit his brother and kissed Rae," Annie informs him.

"Damn. Serves that snotty prick right."

"Who?" Annie asks.

"The brother. Pretty boy has no chill." The derision in Beck's voice is laced with something else, maybe from when Ash slammed Beck's reality TV show the weekend we were all on the yacht last year for my birthday.

I think of Ash's issues with drugs—if Beck only knew—but say nothing.

"He's had a tough season. It's a lot of pressure," I

hear myself say. "You'd like him if you gave him a chance."

"Fortunately, I'll never have to."

Annie lifts a brow. "Anyway, Harrison's back and you guys have made up."

"Not quite."

"I thought he kissed you," Beck interjects. "Then things escalated from PG and you faded to black for our benefit."

"Please don't fade to black," Annie begs.

I roll my eyes. "There might've been some mature situations. In the bathroom," I go on when Annie makes a "give me more" motion with her hands. "Except things are complicated."

Annie's smile broadens. "Tyler and I did complicated. Your damage can't be any worse."

"He's trying to bring down Mischa Ivanov, this business rival of his. The one who burned down his building. The problem is, I'm also trying to play Ivanov's prize club."

Beck whistles, and Annie's jaw drops. "Rae, I agree with Harrison on this one."

"But La Mer is everything I've dreamed of playing."

"You could have fun playing other gigs, couldn't you?" Annie asks.

"I don't know. It hasn't been fun lately," I hear myself say without thinking. "The last six months, it's felt more like phoning it in. Which is a fucking awful thing to say, but I wonder if I've done everything there is to do. Except La Mer."

"So, once you play it, you can check it off your bucket list and take cover?"

Except when Annie says it, it doesn't feel right.

I shake my head. "I don't believe in revenge, but I agree this guy needs to be off the streets. Ibiza would be better off, his patrons would be better off, the music industry too. I'm playing other clubs. I get up in other peoples' businesses in a way Harrison can't."

"Because you're still hoping you two can ride off into the sunset on a yacht together?"

"He doesn't like boats."

"When he got you the yacht last year..."

"He thought I wanted it."

Annie sighs, and even Beck's brows pull together.

"What are you thinking?" I ask. I don't usually solicit input, but next to my cousin, these two are my closest, most trusted friends. And unlike Callie, they understand the complications of living life in the spotlight.

"Queen's gotta help her King," Beck says wryly.

"It's not about Harrison," I insist. "It's a public service. Anything I find, I'll pass on to the police."

"But if it gets you hurt," Annie adds, "I will kill him."

Your first night playing a club is partly a crapshoot—the crowd, the weather, all of it can conspire to make your set a party to remember or one to forget. The second night is when you find out if you've got it.

Tonight for Bliss, I choose a white dress that resembles leather but isn't. It's fitted, but the fabric has a little give so I can move, and it's not as hot in the booth. White sandals top off the look.

"You're coming with me?" I ask Ash as I put the finishing touches on my makeup.

"Think I'll lay low for the evening." He frowns. "All the talk about drugs... I'd rather keep my distance."

Realization hits me. "Understood." I check the edges of my wig to ensure none of my hair shows beneath. "I get that you didn't want to tell Harrison you were buying, but why didn't you tell him what you saw?"

"I'd rather not say. But it would hurt him if he knew."

"I can keep a secret. I can be loyal to you as much as to him."

"Yeah. But you shouldn't have to be." He comes up behind me, and his gaze meets mine in the mirror.

I fold my arms over my chest. "Just tell me one thing—are you talking with the police?"

He nods. "I told them I'd give them all I know. It's not much, but it's compelling."

The reason he knew he was buying Mischa's drugs in a London club still eludes me, but I trust him.

"Fine. Has Harrison said anything about the investigation into your parents?"

"No. Why?"

Fuck. That means Harrison's been shouldering this alone for the better part of a year. "He was looking into it last year, back when he was still trying to buy La Mer from Christian."

I brush past Ash and grab my phone, cursing as I realize I forgot to recharge it after my call with Annie and Beck. "Hey, did you do something to piss off Beck? You seem to have made an impression on him on the yacht last year."

He shoves his hands in the pockets of his shorts, his mouth twisting. "I seem to make terrible impressions on all men."

"That asshole on your team doesn't deserve you. You'll find someone who does."

Ash smirks. "I want someone I don't deserve. Like Harry found."

My chest tightens as I head to the show.

I snap a picture in the limo and post it to social. New habits, but already ingrained.

My fan base has grown and evolved. I can show

up at a venue and find hundreds of people, sometimes thousands, there to see me. It's humbling.

Sometimes it's numbing too.

It's one of the things I wish I could've talked to
Harrison about over the past year. My friends understand the fame, but it's not the same as sharing it
with the man who sees me, challenges me, like no
other.

When I get to the club, there's already a crowd.

I get the owner in a corner. "The drugs sold in
your club. You have to speak out about them."

"I don't know what you're talking about."

I blink. "You told me the other day…"

But then I realize the truth. He won't say a word.
Harrison's right.

By the time I take the stage, I'm already
frustrated.

But I play my set, waiting to be swept up in it as I
change from one track to the next. This club is twice
the size of Debajo, and it's nearly full. The crowd is
loving me.

I should be loving this.

Pressed near the stage is a group in costume. A
girl meets my gaze and dissolves into delighted
screams. My attention pans to a guy dancing near
her, who catches my eye and makes like he's giving
oral.

I turn away, needing a breather that's impossible
while on stage.

My thumb presses the tattoo on my wrist, the backs of my eyes burning.

Feel alive.

Be alive.

Get it together.

I turn back and motion to security. "Vodka soda."

Then I throw myself into the rest of my set. I'm finishing the drink when movement in the far corner of the club catches my eye.

The same guy from before. Selling.

I look over at the manager at the bar. He knows it's happening, and he doesn't even try to stop it.

The woman from the front of the stage is there, buying.

I want to stop her. To say he's bad news. But from here, I can't. I'm the most powerful woman in the room, and I'm helpless.

I finish my set and do selfies with fans. I half wish the woman would come up since she seemed like a big fan. But there's no sign of her.

Unsettled is the only thing I feel.

I'm headed out through the side door when I trip over something soft and lumpy. When I realize what it is, my stomach drops.

It's a body. A person.

Horror rises up as I recognize the woman who was buying inside.

I drop to my knees, feeling for her pulse.

I should call for the club owner, but he won't do anything to cross Mischa.

There's one person I want to call, and I won't even question my reasons for calling him.

When Harrison arrives, Toro driving, I'm still standing with the woman who was passed out near the side entrance of the club. Harrison stalks out of the car and takes in the scene, his expression grim and unusually blank.

It takes a moment for him to speak, and when he does, his voice is rough. "What the fuck happened? Who is she?"

"I don't know who she is. But she overdosed on something." I hold out what I found in her pockets. "I called for the owner after I called you. Management wouldn't let me call an ambulance. They didn't want the overdose traced back to Mischa."

"That doesn't make sense. Tourists overdose all the time. Could be the shit they're dealing is cut with something else. Makes it cheaper to produce and more dangerous to consume."

Harrison feels for her pulse, then looks around. Because we could be seen together, I realize. He's risking everything being here.

It's too late to change it.

We pile her into the back seat to take her to the hospital.

The doctors in Ibiza are used to overdoses, and they smoothly take over the second we bring her inside and establish how we found her. She's in a coma, but I make them promise to let us know when her condition changes.

We head back out to the car, Harrison hanging his head.

Inside, Toro flicks a gaze back before pulling out onto the street. Despite his quiet presence, in that car, it's just the two of us and the awful things we've seen tonight.

"Why did you call me?" Harrison asks.

I swallow hard. "Because you're going after Mischa and I figured you would want to know first-hand what was happening."

But that's not true. I'd planned to tell the police, not Harrison.

Calling him was instinct. Something terrible happened, and he was the person I wanted at my side.

"Señor? Are you all right?"

I look between Toro and Harrison, who nods tightly. Then Toro buzzes up the partition.

"What's going on?" I demand.

"Overdoses are hard. Since I found my parents dead."

Shock slams into me, chased by grief.

He found them?

I assumed it had been a neighbor or someone who worked for them.

Now, I picture a college-aged Harrison bursting in the front door, pulling up at the grotesque sight.

"I'm so sorry."

My eyes burn, my cheeks tingling with wetness.

"Don't, Raegan. It's not your fault."

He's stoic, controlled. Maybe this is how he became that way. Put in a position that left him feeling utterly helpless.

I touch his hair, smoothing my fingers through it. "This man is out there hurting people, and we have to stop him."

He pulls me against him, and my face nestles into his suit jacket. The air between us is tight. With grief, with anger. His arms band around me like steel.

We don't live in a safe world, but his resolve reminds me there are people who care about us. That we live in a world worth fighting for.

When we get to my hotel, I don't move for a long time.

"You can't come upstairs," I whisper, his lapel scratching my lips.

His chest rises and falls rhythmically under my face. "Because of what happened tonight or because you don't want me there?"

I pull back to look up at him through damp eyes. "Both."

If we go up to that room together, it won't only be sex.

It'll be therapy.

No, church.

We'll burn one another down to nothing and roll in the ashes before getting up tomorrow and putting clothes on whatever shambles of form remain. And I can't risk that with him. We both have our own priorities, and they're already dangerously intertwined.

"You deserve love, Harrison. No matter what your parents did, no matter what you did. I wish I could convince you of that, but you need to convince yourself. You deserve to be happy."

"Just not with you."

Fuck, that's unfair. But he's trying to push me away. I can see him now. He hides behind his own walls. Mine are high and protective. His are armored with barbs.

"You walked away from me. I loved you. I wanted to spend every day with you. Every damned hour. When you left, it broke me."

My gaze falls to the crown inked on my wrist. "I wanted to remind myself of your confidence, your belief in me. You taught me that loving is worthwhile, even when you don't get it back. That you can be the person you want to be, even when no one's looking. Especially when no one's looking. I will never forget that."

His jaw works, his firm mouth parting in frustration. "I want you, Raegan. If I could tell you how many nights I've lain awake wanting you...But I don't want to see you hurt anymore. I've caused you enough pain. If you ask me to stop, I'll do it."

I stare at him. He doesn't take no for an answer from anyone, merely finds another way to get what he wants. But the expression on his face is earnest.

Mischa needs to be brought down. Tonight, I understand better than ever why this matters to Harrison, why it's so personal he can't let it go.

But letting him break my heart twice would be foolish and might ruin me.

I shift across his lap and grip the door handle. "Yes. Stop."

I'm out of the car before I can take it back.

11

HARRISON

*G*oing through your dead parents' things is an edifying experience. Strange how processing a person's belongings is shaped entirely by your memories of them.

Those memories have changed shape and color since last year.

Growing up, I swore my parents had all the answers. Until they started arguing at night in hushed tones. I challenged them to leave the business they were in and start fresh on their own. When they died, the guilt crippled me. It was my fault they'd left.

Finding them dead only made it worse. The people I loved and admired were gone, and Sebastian would grow up without parents, and every time I closed my eyes for years, I saw their still, slumped forms and blamed myself.

Now, learning they hadn't really been trying to leave, I should feel as if a weight has been lifted. They weren't innocent. Some people might even go so far as to say they deserved their fate.

Except my need for vengeance on the man who killed them has grown—not because they were saints, but because when Mischa burned Kings to the ground. It wasn't only about them anymore.

He attacked *my* business, the one I built from nothing with my own hands.

The Ivanov family molded my past with cruel, greedy hands.

They won't touch my future.

I'm in the third-bedroom closet, surrounded by boxes, unpacking photos and other items that have sat here since I had them shipped from London.

Some items I toss in a pile to get rid of.

I can't sell their things, so I'll donate them.

When I spot a slim, black lacquered box, my chest tightens. Inside the lid, there's a photo of Ash as a baby. Me holding him with a put-upon smile. I would've been fourteen, I think, and home from school on a break.

My mother never kept her things in a safe. She wouldn't let my father convince her, no matter what beautiful trinkets he bought her. She wasn't a suspicious person. Once she said, "If someone cares enough to take them, they need them more than I do."

The exception was her wedding ring.

I lift it from the case, the gold band slim and smooth in my fingers. There's an inscription I never noticed before. *Through everything.*

I'm surprised it's here. When they passed, I had the funeral home dress them in clothes as different as possible from what they were wearing when I found them. Anything to clear that awful image from my mind. I told the funeral home to bury them with their rings. Yet this one's here.

Footsteps in the hall have me glancing up. As they approach the half-open door, I call, "Natalia. Could you—"

"Not Natalia." Sebastian steps inside. His shorts are forest green, his favorite shade as a child, and his polo shirt is a few shades lighter.

I set the ring back in the box and rise, the box still in my hands. "What are you doing here?"

"Rae told me what happened last night at the bar. The woman who overdosed." His eyes search my face.

"Don't do that," I say, irritated.

"What?"

"Try to see if I've lost it. I'm your older brother. I'm supposed to make sure you haven't lost it."

His lips curve, the ghost of a smile.

"Did you talk to the police?" I ask.

He crosses to the bed, the only place to sit, and sinks into the bedspread uninvited. "Yes."

I clench the box harder. He shouldn't be keeping secrets from me. I'm his damned brother.

"When did I let you down, Sebastian?"

"What do you mean?"

"You don't ask me for anything."

"I've asked you for money. You helped put me through school—"

"I mean anything that's going on in your life. You call me when you get drafted, but when your season goes off the rails... I didn't hear from you once."

He flops back on the bed, insolent as a teenager. "You're the infallible older brother with all the answers. If anyone had a different approach, they were wrong. Our parents thought the sun rose out of your arse whether you gave a shit or not."

My chest tightens. "I told them to leave the business, and when they did, it cost them their lives."

He throws his hands wide. "That's not why I'm angry! I'm angry because I didn't lose two pieces of my family that day—I lost three."

His meaning sinks in, prickles lifting the hairs on my neck.

"I took custody of you, Sebastian. Made sure you had what you needed. Not only food and shelter, but the best schools, the top football coaches." I refused to let him grow up with less than I had.

"I didn't need private school or football coaches. I needed my brother. But he was too busy picking up where they left off."

He shoves himself off the bed and stalks toward the window, avoiding my gaze.

I can feel his anger, but it's the hurt in his voice that shakes me. "I had to provide what they couldn't any longer."

"I grew up without a family, Harry. Being a teenager, figuring out what I wanted to do, who I was... it fucking sucked. Not because they were gone, but because I was alone and I didn't need to be."

Fuck. Maybe in trying to protect my brother, I isolated him. I think of Raegan, how her parents made their choices about what was best for her and only hurt her more.

I rub the box between my hands.

I hope to hell I didn't screw up my brother like that. Or if I did, that he ends up a resilient person like she is.

"I'm glad you kept going," I say at last.

He cuts a look over his shoulder at me. "The other option is worse."

Raegan's words about me thinking I don't deserve love echo in my head.

When I tried to protect her last year, convincing myself it was for the best to leave, I destroyed what was left of our relationship.

Perhaps she's not the only one I've done that with.

My next breath is shallow.

"I need to tell you something. Last year, in the

course of trying to win La Mer from Christian, I learned something about our parents. Information I wish I could forget."

He's across to me in a heartbeat. "What?"

The sunlight streaming in the window is at odds with how I'm feeling, but I force out the words that have lain heavy on my shoulders for the past year.

"They were liars." My voice is tight, and I swallow. "I thought they wanted to get out of Mischa's family business, and I told you as much. But they had no intention of leaving. Everything I did to build this business was for them. To avenge them, to make them... It's meaningless. Perhaps I should get rid of the villa too."

I grab the pile of things, including the velvet box, and toss them in a bag by the door before pacing the room.

"Don't. You like the villa."

"I wanted it because it was theirs," I grind out, rubbing a hand over my face.

He doesn't answer, and I glance back to see him thumbing through the bag.

"You knew them more than I did. Had more time with them. The thing is, we build people up to be what they're not. I did the same with you." He opens the jewelry box and takes out the photo. He smiles, holding it up. "I remember this."

I snort. "You don't. You were all of six months old."

"Yeah, but I remember being safe. Protected. Most of all, loved. By them and by you."

"You don't care that they weren't who we thought?"

He turns over the picture. "I never saw that. I'd rather remember that they loved us."

My chest tightens unbearably. Holding my brother at a distance has been harder than I thought, but safer.

Sebastian straightens, lifts the ring out of the box like I did. "'*Through everything*'." He arches a brow. "Guess they knew life wasn't perfect either." Sebastian shuts the box and sets it on the bedspread. "You won't save this, I will."

I nod. "Sebastian?"

He glances up.

"When did you become an adult?"

"Legally, on my eighteenth birthday. Sexually... far sooner. Though, honestly, I'd take it back if I could."

My chuckle rumbles through my chest, dislodging some of the pain. "Do you want to go through the rest together?"

"Let's get lunch first."

We head back out to the hall.

"You know," he tosses over his shoulder as we head down the hall to the stairs, "I told Rae you didn't deserve her."

I pull up, incredulous. "What? When?"

"Yesterday." He pauses at the top of the steps. "But I was wrong."

I shove my hands in my pockets. "I asked if she wanted me to stop pursuing her."

"Why the fuck did you ask that?"

"Because I didn't think she would say yes!"

He rubs a hand over his face, and for a second, I feel like the little brother.

"It was a bluff."

"No, it wasn't. You meant it, and that's why you're freaking out, because now you have to honor it."

He's right, damn him.

"She's the only woman I can see in my life. The only one I want by my side. She's infuriating and argumentative and sullen and beautiful. I don't know how not to go after what I want, Sebastian."

I get that she's angry, but I never expected the feelings beneath to erode.

Now, the prospect of life without Rae makes me howl.

My brother's mouth twists. "Take it from someone who's been there. Loving something you can't have is better than not loving at all."

12

RAE

*L*ast night, I took a sleeping pill.

It's been three days since the night Harrison and I took the woman to the hospital. I haven't heard anything about her condition. Nor have I heard from Mischa since the meeting when I arrived about my La Mer proposal.

Everything seems to be locked into a holding pattern—save my agitation, which seems to grow.

Since the night at Bliss, I replay finding that woman over and over, when I should be working or sleeping. I can't unsee what I've seen, can't help but wonder how many people have been hurt by Mischa Ivanov.

Today, I'm scheduled to do an interview. There's a multicamera setup on this patio in Ibiza Town, and a few fans have clustered around to watch.

The last interview I did in Ibiza was the start of a

rough period of my life—the reporter called me out on being with Harrison.

I've done dozens since then. I'm never quite comfortable.

"I'm here with Little Queen, who's playing a residency at Bliss in Ibiza this summer."

Cheers go up from the street, and I turn to grin at the fans gathered, which only makes them cheer more.

"You've built quite the following," the interviewer says.

"I'm grateful to every person who listens."

"Why is it important to you?"

"Because we're all individuals going through our own shit."

Her eyebrows lift, and I wonder belatedly if I can swear on this channel.

"What shit"—she sneaks an apologetic look at the camera guy, and I laugh—"are you going through?"

I uncross and recross my legs on the high stool, glad I wore ripped denim and sandals rather than a dress. "The usual. Working on some new songs. Soaking up the sun."

The man I loved is trying to bring down a drug dealer while I'm trying to get said drug dealer to hire me.

I haven't seen Harrison since the night of my show, and that's eating at me too.

But after our call, Annie sent me a picture of

Harrison holding her baby. It hit me hard. Not because I've ever thought of having kids with him. The idea of Harrison as a father seems completely at odds with his mission, his entire ethos.

But is it? Everything he did has been driven by love for the people he cares about. Even if he chose that love over our love.

Before the sleeping pill kicked in last night, I couldn't resist typing out a text that I sent along with the image.

Rae: You better hope this doesn't get leaked publicly. Ovaries will explode.

Harrison replied instantly.

Harrison: Even yours?

I stared at the message for too long. Was he up because he was thinking of me? Thinking of Mischa? Or something entirely unrelated—the direction of interest rates or the last season of the *Great British Bake Off*?

Rae: I'm not maternal.

Harrison: I doubt that very much. But there is a precedent.

Then he sent me a picture of a teenaged Harrison holding a blond baby wrapped in a blanket.

Rae: Wow. Ash looks… innocent. You look as if you'd fight the world for him.

Harrison: I learned early to take no prisoners. Hesitation leads to weakness. Compassion precedes defeat.

I debated before responding.

Rae: That's a good way to make enemies. You'll always be fighting.

Harrison: It's the only way I know how to live.

That was the tragedy.

He taught me how to fight—for myself, for my dreams, for the love I deserve.

But I want him to lay down his weapons.

Another text appeared before I could respond.

Harrison: I never stopped caring.

My heart kicked. Part of me wanted to believe it was true, not only for his sake but for mine.

I fell asleep soon after but woke still thinking of him.

"Something arrived for you before the interview," the reporter says slyly, bringing me back. "Would you like to see it?"

I straighten in my seat, surprised.

One of the crew brings out pink tiger lilies, and I take them, awkwardly shifting to grab the envelope and slide out the card. I read the single phrase written on the white paper.

Take no prisoners.

My body explodes into tingles as if Harrison himself brushed my hair back and whispered the words against my ear.

"You have an admirer. Well, you have lots of them," the interviewer amends, grinning at the crowd. "This looks like a special one."

Awareness has the hairs on my neck lifting despite the heat.

Harrison's watching.

Flowers could be construed as not backing down, but he'd argue they're just for support.

Too bad him being sweet is as destructive as a full-on assault on my body and my heart.

I tuck the card away. If I say I'm seeing someone,

it'll raise suspicion. But when she goes on, my task gets infinitely harder.

"You were linked to Harrison King last year. First in Ibiza, later in LA. Do you think he sent the flowers?"

I turn over my thoughts, knowing he's watching. I shouldn't say anything, but I can't resist. "He's a fighter, not a lover."

"Is that what came between you?"

My smile fades. "A lot of things came between us. But I'm a different person now."

They think I mean a person who wouldn't date Harrison. But that's not it.

I'm a person who can handle the heat. Who can go toe to toe with not only Harrison, but anyone who threatens me and the people I care about.

"What's next for Little Queen?"

"My residency runs another month. And..." An idea clicks into place. "I don't know if I'm allowed to say this." I sweep a coy look over the crowd and see every damn person lean in or bounce on their toes. "I'm working on something special, one night only, at the club everyone comes to Ibiza for."

Screams erupt. Squeals and shouts of "Yes!" and "La Mer!"

"When?" another person hollers when the initial noise dies down.

"I can't talk about it," I say apologetically.

After finishing the show and taking a few selfies

with fans, I change in the venue's bathroom before I head out the back door.

A long, black car pulls up in front of the alley. *Rude.*

I go to move around the back of the car, but it reverses so I can't.

The front window buzzes down to reveal the driver, a severe-looking man in a suit. "Get in."

Russian accent. My spine stiffens.

"Who the hell are you?" Even though I already know.

He holds out a phone showing La Mer's social media page, where everyone is asking when I'm playing. My heart thuds, hiding the first hint of satisfaction in days.

"You tell me where I'm going and I'll get my own ride," I say.

"You want to work for him, you'll get in."

"Once I work for him, maybe I will. Now what's the address?"

I pull up outside La Mer and shift out. For a moment, I wish Harrison was here. But he wouldn't let me come, and I can handle this myself.

A huge security guard meets me at the door, and I start to go through it. He blocks my way and holds out his arms, motioning for me to do the same.

"You're joking."

A brusque headshake.

The impulse to run is still there, but it's the middle of the day in an outdoor venue.

His venue.

I follow instructions, and the man pats me down before jerking his head toward the hallway. I follow him down it, realizing halfway through that I'm holding my breath.

Excitement starts to outweigh the nerves as we emerge into the main area.

It feels like a circus ring.

Or maybe a coliseum.

Bars line the perimeter. The stage is at the center, an altar for revelers to worship at.

The lights are rigged into the sides, a sophisticated network of technology.

"Don't fuck with me."

The cold voice has me whipping around to see Mischa emerge from another corridor. I haven't seen him since the day I went to see him.

"I don't wait around for things to happen. I thought you didn't either," I comment.

He stops in front of me, inches away. I force myself not to back up.

He grins suddenly. "You need the money? You should've kept King around after all."

"Do I look like I need money?" I glance back

toward the sports car I rented. "I've always had a soft spot for this place."

Mischa prowls around me. "Personal memories?"

I think of dancing here with Harrison, him kissing me for the first time. But I say, "This is the biggest gig there is. I fucking want it."

His rasp of laughter scrapes over my skin. "And you will do me a favor by playing here?"

I hold up my phone. "After my interview, you had three hundred comments in an hour asking when I'm playing. By tonight, you'll have a thousand."

"I don't like people forcing my hand."

"Really? I think you do."

"Are you almost finished?" a feminine voice calls from behind me.

I turn to see a familiar blond woman emerge from the same hallway Mischa did.

"We haven't formally met." She wears a smile that's bigger than her companion's but no warmer. A thin veneer of cordiality sheathing a viper's fangs. "I'm Eva."

"Raegan."

"I thought it was Tiny Princess?"

"Little Queen," I correct.

The smile is still in place. "I suppose we have something in common now."

I survey her form in surprise.

"We both survived Harrison King." She holds out a hand. "There's hope for you yet."

Her huge diamond blinks in the light.

"Congratulations. Is this new?"

"Just this week," she confirms. "I trust you haven't seen Harrison in some time?"

I shrug. "Why would I?" It's a bad idea to let on that we've been talking. Or fucking. Mischa might misconstrue that as us getting back together, which would mean my loyalties might have shifted.

"But you've seen his brother. You went to an event together."

I turn to face Eva, new wariness setting up in my gut.

"I saw Sebastian recently in London too. A few months ago. He joined some friends in a VIP room."

The pieces click into place.

This bitch is what Ash wanted to keep from Harrison. She pushed the drugs on Ash.

"Sounds like a party," I say, matching my smile to hers.

"Too bad you missed it."

My pulse is heavy against my ribs, either from the thrill of this place or my hatred of these people. "What would be too bad is you missing out on me playing here."

Mischa's shrewd eyes narrow on me. "Why is that?"

"Because your family has been in this business a long time." I purposely don't allude to the drugs. "Do you know what that means?"

"It means I am powerful."

"It means you're the past. I'm the future."

I sense the surprise in him that I would dare to speak to him this way. It's an opening. One no person in their right mind would use.

Take no prisoners.

Mischa is like Harrison in some ways—egotistical, demanding. But without all of Harrison's graces.

So, I know how to provoke him.

I turn back to the venue, sweeping my gaze over the dance floor. "Men who build theaters like to adorn them with gold and velvet to trick the audience into believing the venue is the spectacle. But no matter how comfortable the chairs, how gilded the balconies, it's still only a blank canvas. A theater is only as good as its performers." I close my eyes, take a deep breath of the sunlight and the fresh air. This place will transform at night, become something else, like I do. "I can't tell you how many people have tried to keep me off stages like this one. But they won't."

Mischa watches me like a predator surveying its prey. "And why is that?"

I step closer, my heart hammering against my ribs.

The man before me is dangerous. As skilled as Harrison at business, more talented at manipulation, without the reservations about hurting people.

But I can be dangerous too.

"Because when I'm up there?" I nod my chin toward the stage. "They can't fucking look away."

Mischa's nostrils flare. Blue eyes glow like cold embers, dragging down my body. The top and jeans cover most of my skin, but under his attention, I feel bare.

Blood pounds in my veins, fear and adrenaline. I'm no longer chasing. I'm being chased.

Eva knows it too. She's at his side in an instant, her arm threading possessively through his.

"Your manager has my rates and terms," I say to Mischa once his gaze returns to mine. "I look forward to hearing from you."

I haven't won, but as I square my shoulders and head for the exit, I know I've done something very brave or very foolish.

13

HARRISON

I've never watched a movie over again in my life, but I'm watching Rae's interview for the third time.

The moment the flowers come in and she reads the card, I see it.

Her lips curve the tiniest bit.

Fuck me.

I'm a fucking teenager sending his date a corsage.

A smile.

The texts yesterday out of the blue, which mean she's thinking of me.

It's like the tiniest interaction with her, the slightest tease of emotion, is my oasis in the desert.

I'm taking a break from entertaining guests at Debajo, which is still packed a year after Raegan took on the challenge of reinventing it. The DJ tonight isn't her, but he has the near-capacity crowd captivated nonetheless.

Spending eight months on opposite sides of the globe was one thing. But now she's here, and I can as easily ignore her as I can ignore my own need for oxygen.

She asked me to back down. I won't force myself on her, but I won't stop protecting her. I won't stop loving her.

Earlier in the week, she called me when she found that woman after her set. I'm glad she did. Even if I can't shake the feeling of seeing that crumpled form, even if it brought up memories of my parents' deaths. I got to hold her in the back of the car, see her eyes damp with the tears she never lets fall.

It made me realize something...

Raegan's strength is my damn weakness.

My phone rings.

"King," I shout over the music as I rise from the leather bench.

The voice on the other line belongs to my investigator in London. "Figured you'd want to hear about the sting police tried to run on Mischa's venue here last night."

I excuse myself from the VIPs in my booth—a handful of investors, plus twin celebrity actresses.

"What happened?" I demand, pressing my other

hand to my ear to listen over the music as I cross the catwalk and head for the stairs.

Security holds the door, and the next second, I'm in the quiet hallway leading to the VIP room.

The man on the phone sighs. "A source suggested there was a big deal going down. What they found was a poor cousin of that. And the guy involved... some small-time dealer with no links to Ivanov."

Either the police fucked up, or Mischa knew they were coming.

I pinch the bridge of my nose. "A tourist ODed here the other night and nearly died. Not uncommon, but the drugs were cut with something. Doctors wouldn't disclose, but it was something bad."

He hesitates.

"Our surveillance of Ivanov saw a woman arrive at La Mer earlier today shortly after Mischa did."

I shake my head, impatient. "And?"

"It was Miss Madani."

My hand has a death grip on the phone.

"We couldn't get close enough to hear what they were meeting about, so we can only speculate—"

"I fucking know what they were meeting about."

I hang up and drop into an armchair in the VIP room. It's quiet tonight, just the bartender who left the moment I waved him away.

How the hell could she visit Mischa?

I want to storm her hotel suite again. I'll lock her up in my villa until this is all over. But something tells me she won't be nearly as welcoming as she was last time, and that landed me with a bruised cheek for two days.

Since my brother and I went through our parents' belongings, I've been wondering how much damage I did unnecessarily to people I love.

Maybe if I can destroy Mischa, I'll have another shot with Rae too.

I replay the video of her getting the flowers and watch her try not to smile once more.

"Huh. I knew you were getting old, but napping? For real?"

I straighten and open my eyes to see a welcome sight. My right-hand woman stands in the doorway with her hands on her waist.

"Leni. Christ."

"Evening, boss."

I rise and cross to my friend, clasping her in a hard embrace.

"If I'd known you were this strung-out, I would've come sooner."

"Why didn't you?"

"Told you. Vacation. My cabana boy licked the sand out of my toes and—"

"I'm sorry I asked." I hold up a hand, and she grins.

I cross to the door, shutting it to ensure we have extra privacy. "We need to take Mischa down."

"His goons are selling outside. Pulled a knife on me, but I chased them off."

Alarm works through me. "You're joking."

"Nope. I knew one of 'em from last summer and told him what I'd do with his balls if he tried selling here again. New manager pissed himself when he saw the blade."

I think of the guy Leni put in place once the club was made profitable last year and she accompanied me to LA. I vow to replace him immediately.

"It's not only about Kings, Leni. His reach has broadened. He's in America. In London. He's running drugs through other owners' clubs here, forcing them to turn a blind eye, then blackmailing them after. Interpol has been working to link him to narcotics activities, but they've cocked it up."

She leans in. "So, what do we do?"

"We need to strike him close to home. Everywhere his parents built up, he's well protected. Hundreds of employees without contracts who get fed only the bare minimum info. Whom he can deny having any knowledge of if it comes up. It's the perfect business. But he's not as smart as his parents, which means there's an opening. We need options, and we need to move fast."

"You want to play cop, Harrison? Never figured you for the polyester-and-a-badge sort."

I narrow my gaze. "Raegan came to Ibiza to book La Mer."

Leni's eyes round. "Oh shit."

Her expression says she knows exactly what that means—that the woman I love is working with the most dangerous man I know.

"She's met with Mischa. Twice," I bite out.

"Have you told her not to?"

"Of course."

She grimaces. "Bad idea."

"What?" I demand.

"Let's see. You guys broke up last year—"

"Separated."

"Whatever—because you were an unreasonable prick after Mischa went all pyro on your new project."

"So, a Russian madman responsible for my parents' deaths burns down a ten-million-dollar project and I'm unreasonable?"

"With her, yes. She's more likely to do something if you tell her not to."

I drop my head in my hands and tug on my hair hard enough my scalp aches. "What is it with women?"

"Brains, empathy, and pussies," she fires back. "It's worth taking the time to figure them out. Don't go anywhere." She claps me on the shoulder as she rises and crosses to the bar, where she grabs the good whisky and pours a single glass on ice.

"None for you?" I demand as she brings it back to me.

"I'll come back for mine. First, I'm going to go talk your manager down from the ledge."

14

RAE

"*Y*ou buy those?"

I look up from my computer as Ash enters the suite, juggling a ball between his knees.

"Buy what?" I ask.

"The flowers."

I look at the lilies from Harrison that I've moved around the hotel room no less than five times. "No. They were a gift."

After doing the interview yesterday and going to La Mer to see the Russian homewrecker and his happily wrecked now-fiancée, I'm trying to enjoy a day to myself.

Instead, I'm questioning whether I made a grave miscalculation by going after Mischa so aggressively.

"We have company," Ash goes on with a grin.

I straighten in my seat at the kitchen table,

tugging on the hem of my threadbare tank top. *Is Harrison here?*

Ash holds the door, and the guy from the gala, Gavin, follows him in.

"Hey." The man gives me a wave every bit as casual as his messy-on-purpose brown hair and his easy grin.

If he recognizes me from the event, he doesn't let on. Or maybe Ash told him we're nothing.

"Excuse us." I grab Ash and tug him out to the patio, shutting the door. "This a good idea?"

"Have you seen him?" He tosses an appreciative look at the man, who's perusing the coffee table magazines. "Plus, he came here for me."

I lift my hands. "Last time, the way he acted sent you spinning out. You deserve someone great, Ash, and I don't like how he treated you."

"S'alright," he murmurs. "Gavin is about to make it up to me." He ruffles my hair. "But thanks."

I watch him head inside, grab the man's wrist, and drag him down the hall. Conflicted feelings collide in my chest. I want to see Ash happy, but with someone who deserves him.

Sex is one thing, but if he's trying to hide feelings behind it...

Maybe it's nothing. Maybe this guy won't hurt him again, or maybe Ash can keep physical separated from the emotional.

Before I can decide what to do, my phone rings

on the table. I lunge for it, my stomach flipping as I see it's an unknown number.

Possibly Mischa.

"Yeah?" I answer.

"Rae. It's Leni."

My brows shoot up as I close out of the Ableton Live software on my computer. "Oh, hey."

"We've had a little problem at Debajo. I need you."

I'm already visualizing flames like the night Harrison was dragged from his bed to find Kings a pile of smoldering char. "What kind of problem?"

"Our talent for tonight isn't going to make it. He's too stoned to play."

Disbelief rises up. Not because it's the first time in history a DJ has been inebriated on stage, but because Harrison could've had the decency to call me himself.

Just because I told him to back off pursuing me doesn't mean I wouldn't have enjoyed him asking me to come back to Debajo. A little begging would have been nice.

Now that I picture it, him on his knees, looking up at me like I'm his entire damned world, even as he prepares to wreck me...

Focus, dammit.

"Listen, I know Harrison has a problem with people using substances, but you might have to compromise this time—"

"No, Raegan, I mean he's too stoned to play. Like, I'm looking at him, and he's a mumbling pile on the floor." Pause. "Here. I'm waving his hand at the phone. 'Hello, Little Queen. Will you cover my set? I'm a fucking mess.'"

I press a hand to my face, already feeling like crawling back into bed. "It's my day off."

"That's going around. Tag, you're it." She laughs. "I promise it'll be more fun than the place you're playing all summer."

"Bliss has been great," I argue.

"But it's not home."

Home. As I remember the stage, the VIP room, the staff, a familiar longing tugs at me.

"Is there a theme?"

"*The future is you.*"

I make a face. "Sounds like a bad yearbook title."

She laughs. "You got something better? We have time to change it and let everyone know."

Leni's someone I respect independent of Harrison. Plus, it's not her fault he didn't call me himself, and I'm not going to give another woman shit for asking for help just because her boss should've done it.

I consider the highly produced shows I've been doing at Bliss and my lips twitch. "I have an idea."

I fill her in, sending an image to go with my description.

She's quiet for a long time but finally chuckles. "Let's do it."

After hanging up, I head down the hall.

Groaning and panting drift through Ash's closed door. I don't bother telling him where I'm headed.

I go to my room and pull the closet door wide.

"Thanks for the ride," I say, leaning forward from the back seat.

"My pleasure, señorita. You need to come visit."

"I will," I promise. "Tell Natalia I'm making her a crocheted doll."

I shift out of the car, the trench coat wrapped around me mostly for Toro's benefit.

There's a line around the block, and the marquee reads: "COME AS YOU ARE." As I approach the string of patrons, I get a look at some of the outfits. There's more skin than clothing.

For once, it's not fancy lingerie-inspired outfits. It's simple. Nude bandeau tops and miniskirts for the women. A few even have nipples drawn on. The men are in shorts or speedos, a few painted flesh tones.

I can't help grinning.

Leni, what did you do?

I head in the back, headphones and drive in my

bag. Security's stoic faces break as they spot me. I fist-bump one guy.

"You're overdressed," he comments as he holds the door for me.

"Not for long," I toss over my shoulder as I head to the VIP room.

Leni's waiting for me at the VIP bar. She's dressed more like security in head-to-toe black. It's early, and a handful of staff are back here, including the bartender, who nods at me in recognition. I return the gesture.

"Cam, can I get a—"

"Vodka soda coming up."

I grin, turning back to Leni.

"See? Like coming home," she says.

Maybe she's right. It already feels better. As if parts of me are waking up. I remember how hungry I was only a year ago, how every show was shiny and new and a chance to do what I loved.

"How'd you get a thousand people to wear skin with three hours' notice?" I ask.

She shrugs. "Convincing young, beautiful, drunk people to get naked? Not that hard. And I told them Little Queen would be here to show them the way."

I reach for the belt of my trench coat and shrug out of it.

Cam the bartender is at my side with the vodka soda, but he freezes when I toss the coat on a nearby chair. "Jesus."

"Venus," I correct.

"*Birth of Venus*, actually," Leni goes on, scanning me admiringly.

I catch a glimpse of myself in the mirror over the bar. The custom lace bodysuit matches my skin tone. I bought it to wear under another costume, but I figured tonight called for something simple. The effect is definitely provocative.

On my feet are nude platform sandals. My blond hair is straight, hanging in slow waves to cover my breasts. My eyes are lined dark, and my lips are sheer.

It's more than hot.

And sure, maybe I wanted to push Harrison's buttons, to remind him he can't jerk me around anymore without getting jerked right back.

Sue me.

I reach for my vodka soda and take a congratulatory sip.

"Can I get you anything else, Raegan? Miss Queen? Fuck," Cam mumbles.

Leni pinches his cheek. "Sweetie. You're cute. But if the boss comes down here, you're gonna have to put those eyes back in, or he'll rip them out and keep them."

Cam gulps and heads back to the bar.

Leni laughs silently. "You do look fucking incredible."

"Thanks. I'm missing one thing." I reach into my

bag, pulling out my headphones. I loop them around my neck, the cord secured. "There."

She shakes her head.

"What?" I prompt.

"Just deciding if I should call Harrison or wait for him to find out."

My smile dies. "He doesn't know I'm here?"

Her brows shoot up. "Honey, I didn't ask the boss. Think he has a business dinner tonight. Maybe he'll swing by after."

Shit. I assumed Harrison was in on this and had his own reasons for not calling me. But he didn't know...

I catch sight of myself in the mirror once more.

It's too late to worry about what he'll think about it. Two thousand people in the next room need entertainment. And I won't let them, or the staff of the place that made me, down.

15

RAE

I take the stage to deafening applause.

I play some experimental shit. Some stripped down remixes, even the song I was working on that I can't get quite right.

The crowd is dancing and loving and living, and I'm in it with them. My hands are in the air, and I'm losing myself in the music.

Leni's right. This feels like home.

I might even know how to fix this track now.

I'm hearing the changes in my head, committing them to memory when awareness jerks me back to the present.

The champagne bucket appears at my side, full of waters.

I put off responding for thirty seconds. A minute. Even change the tracks once without giving in to the desire to look up.

When I can't hold back anymore, I lift my gaze to the VIP.

Harrison King is wearing a tuxedo, bracing both hands on the railing. His perfect jaw is set, firm lips pressed into a hard line, his hair mussed as if he caught himself running a hand through it.

His eyes are locked on me.

In a room full of pagans dancing underground...

He's a god.

And he's pissed.

Part of me wishes I could tell him I didn't do this to mess with him. Even though there's nothing he can do. He can't very well drag me from the stage.

Though the idea makes me shiver.

We can't be together in public because I can't have Mischa thinking we're an item again.

And in private, it's too risky to my heart.

But like this, I can touch him without touching him.

We're surrounded. It's the most dangerous place to be, and the safest.

Since he walked into my hotel room, I've been a mass of emotions. Wanting, aching, longing, regretting.

I can wish he didn't leave me, but I can't change that he did. But I wouldn't rewind time and erase what happened between us. I wouldn't even erase the hurried sex in his bathroom last week.

The more I stare at him, the more I realize...

I wouldn't erase a thing.

We never should have been, and that only makes me cling more determinedly to what we were. What we are. Even if we're not a couple and I'm not hoping for a happily ever after with this man, something between us is alive and teeming, now, in this basement.

So, I play for him.

I choose the songs, tracks that will move the crowd and fit the stripped-down theme of "Come As You Are," but that also fit us. I create a new set on the fly, my fingers moving as fast as my mind.

This set is my own personal mixtape for my fuck-hot ex.

He watches like he knows it.

My body is on fire. After a couple of drinks, coupled with the power of this place, I could touch myself right here.

I could come from it.

I could beg for it.

Does he feel the same way?

He's still watching. He hasn't looked away.

Take no prisoners.

I flip him off, then run my tongue along the side of my finger. I swear his eyes darken.

In the VIP booth overhead, he widens his stance, adjusts his pants, then rubs the bulge in the front.

My throat dries.

I change the track to the one I made last

summer, the one I told him he could jerk off to and think of me.

His movements stop as if he knows what I'm doing.

It's a filthy dare he can't possibly take me up on.

Maybe it's the night or the frustration between us, or maybe I'm just that goddamned good, because the silver on his belt flashes in the light as he flicks it open.

Holy shit.

Then his hand is inside. He starts again, slower.

The expression on his face...

It's the hottest fucking thing I've seen in my life.

I'm a live wire now, my skin prickling as heat rushes over me.

My core throbs. On stage, I can't slide a hand between my thighs without being seen, but I want to rub on Harrison, on my own fingers, on anything.

This club is more than a third wheel in this transaction. It's part of both of us, one we won't ever give up.

For the next song, I split my attention between the partiers and Harrison. If I stare up too long, someone will figure out what's happening.

That the most fully dressed man in this place is stone-cold sober and fucking his hand.

Every movement of his arm, his jacket, feels like he's tugging on a string wrapped around my core.

I'm so fucking turned on in this moment, I think I might come for real.

His jaw is tight, his hand working his cock like he's my dream fantasy come to life. I'm breathless, my reckless smile impossible to hold in when I pick up the pace of the track.

His gaze narrows, but he does the same with his strokes.

The music moves every person in this club, but he's moving me.

I can tell when he's getting close. I can't look away.

I want to watch him come.

I want to *feel* it.

His head tips back.

He's close.

His hips jerk. Once. Twice. Then he groans—I can't hear it over the pounding bass, but I see it.

When he comes, I *do* fucking feel it. The wave grips me, and I reach for the desk in front of me to steady myself as if I'm coming too.

His unsteady breathing is mine.

When confetti rains down from the ceiling, I realize this is the best time I've had in a long time. Maybe ever.

It's because of Harrison, but also because of this place. It does feel like home.

The crowd is chill and happy, content to take selfies at Debajo with me, with each other. Then the crowd parts, and my breath catches.

Harrison King walks toward me, his tuxedo jacket unbuttoned and his mouth pressed in a hard line.

When he reaches me, I say, "I thought it wasn't a good idea to be seen together in public."

"It's not, which is why you're in trouble."

He's cool, cold even, as he gestures for me to go ahead and follow security. I head down the hall toward the VIP room. Leni's there, along with the bartender. Harrison shuts the door before turning to face us.

"Whose bright idea was this?" His voice is deadly calm.

"I called her," Leni admits. "We had a cancellation last minute. And Cam's a terrible fucking DJ."

The bartender ducks his head.

"Cam?" I call. "Mr. King could use a whisky."

He fixes one immediately, bringing the glass over. His gaze slides to my legs, and his throat bobs.

Harrison sends the guy scurrying away with a look.

"Cam, I'll drink the whisky." I cross to the bar and take it from him before sipping the golden liquid.

Harrison paces the room. "Mischa isn't supposed

to know we're talking. Tonight you all but announced it."

"We announced that Debajo had an opening," Leni cuts in, "and a former DJ in residence picked up the slack for an impromptu—and a fucking fantastic, might I add—show."

Adrenaline surges through me again. It was fantastic.

"You're the one making this worse by marching her down here," Leni goes on.

Harrison's gaze finds mine.

If Leni knew that her boss had jerked off to me upstairs...

"To be fair," I say, the whisky heating my stomach, "it probably looked as if you were marching me here to chew me out. Which is apparently what's happening."

"There's a car for you out front," Harrison says.

My breath hitches. He's sending me away? I told him to back off, but after what happened upstairs, it feels like a slap in the face.

Without a word, I turn to leave.

I make my way through the halls and out to the parking lot. A sleek, black limo is waiting. I get in, and the car pulls away. I half expect it to circle the block and return for Harrison or do some other covert maneuver. But I'm disappointed when it continues straight down the road.

A few minutes later, it turns the opposite direction of my hotel.

"Excuse me, where are we going?"

The man doesn't answer.

Nerves dial up, and I pull out my phone to call Harrison. But before the ringtone sounds, I realize where we're headed.

The car parks at the beach, and I get out. The familiar sound of waves crashing along the shore greets me. I scan the nearly empty parking area for Harrison's car, the knot in my chest loosening when I spot it.

He's already there.

On the beach.

I take off my shoes at the edge of the beach and walk to him, the sand slipping between my toes. He meets me halfway. He's barefoot, his waistcoat unbuttoned. The breeze blows his hair, and his eyes glow like blue coals in the dark.

I spot a piece of confetti stuck to his jacket sleeve.

"Classy," I murmur as I pick it off.

I barely have time to look back up before he drags me against his hard body.

"I know you went to see Mischa. *Again*."

I drop the shoes and my bag to fold my arms in the little space between us. "And I know you fucked your hand until you popped like a bottle of Dom at a bachelorette in the middle of Debajo. So, we all have secrets."

He shakes me hard, anger and fear clouding another emotion in his eyes. "I'm tempted to tie you to my damn bed just to keep you safe."

We're so close that his lips rub across mine when he bites out the words.

"Is that the only reason?" I murmur.

He hauls my lips to his. It's possessive and desperate, and I want to fight him, but not as much as I want to hold him close.

He backs me across the sand. His hands cup my face, the initial demand giving in to something earnest and full of longing. I jerk in surprise when my heels hit the water and the waves lick at my ankles.

He pulls back an inch. His eyes are as deep as the sea, every bit as tortured. "I won't let you pretend this is all I want from you."

I swallow, my heart racing as I grip his wrists. "What do you want?"

"That first night I arrived," he mutters, his voice oddly rough, "I didn't ask Sebastian if he fucked you. I asked him if he loved you."

Shock slams into me, tickling starting deep in my stomach like the tickling from the waves against my legs as he continues.

"I couldn't bear the idea. When I saw the photo of you two at the event, it destroyed me. I tried to tell myself I would stay away if he was what you wanted."

His thumb strokes the tattoo on the inside of my wrist. His words course through my veins, leave me shuddering. We're up to our hips now, the water tugging at the fabric of his tuxedo pants. Harrison doesn't notice, or if he does, he doesn't care.

"Because I love you. I loved you first. And no matter what happens, dammit, I'll love you last."

I've seen Harrison King ruthless. I've seen him angry.

I've never seen him desperate.

I'm a different woman than I was a year ago. I'm stronger and weaker. I hurt more and I love more. I didn't think it was possible to be both of those things.

He taught me how.

We're connected in a way that will never end. Out here, where I feel as if I met the real Harrison King for the first time, I can't deny it.

I shove off his jacket and toss it toward the shore.

"You missed," he murmurs against my open mouth.

"Did not."

I wind my arms around his neck as he reaches beneath the water to cup my ass, molding me to the hardness between his thighs.

His mouth closes over mine. It's hungry and powerful, and he pulls my bottom lip between his teeth and bites down until I gasp.

I slip my hand under the water, and when I close

it around that blazing hot hardness, he groans. The sound is primal and raw and goes straight to my core. I massage him, lifting up on my toes to get a better angle, and his hold on my ass tightens.

The sea tries to drag us away, but Harrison is my anchor. Steady. Relentless.

"Tell me you love me," he rasps against my ear.

Before I met him, I never let anyone in. It wasn't living, not really. But the way I felt about him, I was open. Raw.

"I loved you once. More than I thought I could love another person." The words stick in my throat, and his fingers still on the zipper at the back of my bodysuit.

"Then love me again." He leans his forehead against mine.

My heart squeezes. "Harrison..."

I understand why he left the way he did. That doesn't mean I'm ready to start down this path once more. I have the career I want, friends I care about, a life I built myself. When he vanished from it last year, I realized how deep in me he'd been.

I could say that I want to love him, but the world is fucked up. That while I'll stand shoulder to shoulder with him and stare down the devil, I'm afraid to do that with my heart on a string attached to his.

I can be brave, but not when everything I am is tangled up in him.

His jaw clenches. "Until you do, I'll love enough for both of us."

He's holding out hope. I don't know if it's well founded or completely foolish, but I can't help admiring him for it.

I reach for his pants.

He exhales his frustration but presses aside the panel of my outfit. The water tickles my bare skin, and I gasp as he brushes his fingers where I'm already hot and wet.

"I want you in my bed," he murmurs, playing with my slickness. "I want you in my life."

My nails dig into the muscles of his shoulders, the shirt spattered with drops of spray. He presses a finger inside me, and I moan into his mouth.

All my resolve flees, chased away by his words and the rhythm of his finger. I'm get wetter, even under the cold water.

His touch, his words, it all hurts in a way that's so damn good. Because I can't deny it, just like I couldn't deny it a year ago.

This is coming home.

The realization flips a switch, and suddenly, I'm the demanding one.

Every second he's not inside me is too long.

I reach into his underwear for his cock, thick and hard. I wrap my fingers around him, rub my thumb over his crown.

"Raegan... fuck."

He lifts me effortlessly, and I hitch my legs around his hips. His cock presses where I'm aching. I take a breath, change the angle, and he slides inside in an endless stroke.

He's everywhere. His big hands hold me, his cock fills me. His mouth finds mine, and it's like he's finally home, too. There's nothing gentle about what we're doing, and I drag my nails across his skin, mark him.

For tonight, he's mine. I want him to know it.

He moves fast, our mouths still pressed together. The world is spinning around us, the faintest hint of dawn teasing the sky.

He's me. We're inseparable. There's nothing but us and the water washing over our slick skin.

His rough breathing falls on my lips. "Only you. Always you."

His conviction has my heart swelling against my ribs.

The ocean ebbs and flows around us, but Harrison sets his own pace. One for us.

When we come, the sea trembles.

16

HARRISON

*I*t's possible to fall in love anywhere. But here, in the dark, I understand why it's possible to fall here.

She's floating on her back, and I'm holding her by the hand, both of us swaying gently with the waves.

I keep touching her, but it's leisurely and not desperate like before.

I could touch her forever. The curves of her body, its secrets.

When I saw her tonight, I was pissed. And proud.

She's stronger than I ever gave her credit for. This past year, she's gotten stronger still.

My Queen.

I understand why she's wary with her heart. She was before I met her, and now she has reason to be. I gave her reason to be.

"I realized something tonight." My voice cuts through the rhythmic sounds of the beach.

Rae turns toward me, shifting so her feet are rooted in the sand once again.

I tuck a wet piece of hair gently behind her ear. "If Mischa keeps us apart, he's already won. I don't want to keep you at a distance."

She exhales but doesn't answer.

The water flows around us, between us.

"I found my mother's wedding ring the other day. Sebastian and I did, technically. It says, 'Through everything.'" I don't know what they went through, what choices they made. But God, did they love one another."

"You envy them," she reads.

"I respect them. Because I know how fucking hard it is," I admit, threading my fingers through hers. "Last year, my entire past was called into question. If my parents weren't good people, why the fuck should I be? I didn't deserve more. I didn't deserve you. After Kings burned, the only thing I could see a path to was vengeance. I thought I was doing the right thing, the noble thing. I thought I could win you back when it was over. But in trying to save our future, I gave it away before it had begun."

Her troubled eyes search mine. "Your past can only define you if you let it. If there's a chance for us —if," she goes on as if she can feel my jaded heart leap, "we need to be equals, Harrison. You can't make decisions without me."

She presses up on her toes, her full lips coaxing mine. I taste her, the faintest hint of my favorite whisky, but under it is strength. Resolution.

When I pull back, I murmur, "You're a force."

"So are you. Unafraid of jerking off in a tux with a club full of witnesses."

My lips curve to match hers. "You enjoyed that."

I recall how she looked on stage, daring me with her eyes, full lips parting with appreciation when I started.

"Not nearly as much as you did." Her teeth flash white in the dark.

My laughter rumbles through my chest. God, I love this woman. More than I knew I could love anything.

"A cottage," she says.

My brows rise. "A cottage?"

"Somewhere quiet. With a lake. No paparazzi. No work. That's where we'll go when this is all over."

"Ahhh," I say, getting into the possibility. "No internet either."

"But how will you watch *Great British Bake Off*?"

"Unnecessary," I contend as I stroke the back of her hand. "We'll pack our bags—"

"I own *one*—"

"Which I'll buy to replace the god-awful one you have. We can walk Barney in the mornings—"

"Mornings?"

I splash her, and she laughs in protest.

"Early afternoon," I concede when her laughter dies. "Though you won't be playing any late gigs, so you won't need to sleep in."

"I see. And what will I be doing?"

"Swimming. Reading. Me."

Her dark eyes search mine. "It's one thing to fantasize about it, another thing to do it."

I have a ton of work to do to win back her trust. I dug myself a deeper hole than I knew, but she's worth it. She's worth everything.

"I'm taking you on a date," I decide. "Dinner tomorrow. I might not find a taco truck, but it'll be the next best thing. I'll answer anything you ask me. We can talk about the future. And I want you to move back in with me," I go on as her brows pull together. "I'll line up additional security. I hate knowing you're on my island and under some other man's roof."

She trails a hand along the surface of the water, lips curving. "Maybe it's *my* island now."

Fuck. She's a different woman than the one I fell in love with. An even stronger, more fascinating one.

"Come back to me, Raegan. Nothing is the same without you."

It's a minute, an eternity, as I wait her out.

"We can try."

The knot in my chest loosens a degree. But when she starts toward the shore, I catch her hand.

"I need to go back to the hotel tonight," she says.

"Not yet. One more time."

Raegan's the one to run her fingers through my wet hair and rub her swollen lips on mine.

This time when I drag her against me, I'm not thinking of yesterday.

I'm thinking of tomorrow.

17

HARRISON

a shadow falls over me as I hang up my call.

"You look awfully cheerful this morning."

I look up from my café table down at the marina and gesture to the chair opposite. Sebastian drops into it.

"My roommate came home around five this morning," he goes on. "Know anything about that?"

I stretch out my legs, picturing Raegan crawling into her bed sore after the night we had at the beach. "A gentleman never tells."

"Right. I trust from the phone call that you were ordering new testicles to replace the ones Raegan's been carrying in her pocket."

"I was arranging additional security for Raegan and myself." Two for Raegan, two for me.

"Where's my security?"

"Even I can't afford what it would take to have trained ex-military mind your arse once they realized how irritating you are," I gripe.

He rolls his eyes. "Well, I'm glad things are going well between you."

"Some things are still unresolved." She's guarding her heart, and as frustrating as it is, I can't blame her. "But I will do whatever it takes to keep her with me."

Starting with a date tonight, where I will prove how committed I am to our future.

The waitress delivers my coffee, and I gesture to Ash, who orders one too.

A notification buzzes on my phone—a shipment notification for Sawyer's AI. One is destined for London, one for Tokyo, and the third for Debajo here in Ibiza.

I hold up the phone so my brother can see it.

"Nightclub robots?" he demands. "Do they twerk?"

"You're in a good mood too," I observe. It's rare that we can have such a mild conversation, and I'm not foolish enough to believe one heart-to-heart over our dead parents' things erased years of tension. "You sleep like the dead. Which means if you were up when Raegan returned, you had company. Who is she?"

His smile fades. Sebastian flexes his hand on the table. "It wasn't a she."

The waitress returns with his coffee, giving me a few beats to study him. When she leaves, he takes a slow sip, holding my gaze over the rim.

It's a surprise, and also not. I had a suspicion my brother wasn't as enthusiastic about the opposite sex as I was, but he's never said as much, and I've never made it my duty to pry. Perhaps I should've.

Perhaps this was part of why his teenage years were so hellish to suffer through alone.

"Who is he?" I ask evenly.

My brother shifts in his seat, scanning the street behind me. "Another bloke from my club. It was a tough season. Gavin was there for me when I let my team down, reminding me I'm not defined by my performance on any given day. It's easy to forget when you're hounded by management and fans, every mistake hung out for everyone to see."

"Is he good enough for you?"

Sebastian's brows shoot up. "That's not the first question I expected from you."

"Well, it's the one I have."

He shakes his head. "Trust me. He's good. We were still up when Raegan got back..." Then he looks guilty, as if questioning what he should say in front of me.

"I didn't mean in bed."

He rubs a hand over his neck. "I don't know what it is or isn't. We haven't put labels on it. But until we do, the team can't know."

I stare out over the pedestrians strolling the street. I wish he'd confided in me sooner. "If you decide it's something, you'll tell the team?"

He frowns. "I don't know, Harry. People will talk."

"People will always talk."

He shifts forward, rising, and I lay a hand on his arm before he can. I can't help feeling protective of him.

"I don't want them talking about you, but if they do? I'll put them right."

"Send an army of twerking robots after them," he replies, deadpan.

I laugh, and he joins in after a moment.

We'll get through this. I feel that possibility for the first time.

A call comes in, and the name lifts my spirits more.

"Hello, love," I say when I answer. "My brother is with me. Thought I'd let you know before you start talking about how good I was last night."

It's Sebastian's turn to snort.

"So, please, don't be shy. Let's set the record straight on which King is the best lover. I'll even put you on speaker." I hit the button, grinning, but there's nothing at the other end.

Finally, Raegan's voice comes over the phone. "Harrison, the woman we took from Bliss to the hospital after she overdosed? I asked the doctors to let me know if her condition changed, but hadn't heard anything, so I went by the hospital. I figured we could find out if she saw anything that would help us."

I don't love the idea of her playing investigator, but I go with it. "And?"

"Her condition changed. She's dead."

RAE

After playing Debajo and spending the rest of the night with Harrison, I was riding a high until I got word of the woman's death.

She was a stranger, but Harrison's fury and grief over her death proves how far he's come since I met him. I can't picture the man he is now turning his back on people, even ones he has no responsibility for.

But when Harrison called a meeting for Leni, Ash, himself, and me at the villa, he was in control once again.

"He's getting reckless, pushing bad supply through clubs that don't even belong to him," Harrison says, seated at the head of the table. "I want you all to be careful."

Leni devours the spread Natalia fixed for us on

short notice—fresh sandwiches on ciabatta with pastries for dessert. Plus wine, which Ash avoids looking at.

"Fine. So we lie low," Leni says. "All I care about is that Mischa stays away from your venues. But what are you going to do?"

"Find a way to stop him. I spoke with Christian," Harrison says. "He's out of the game, and even he won't cross Mischa. But there has to be someone who'll talk. We just haven't found them yet."

Harrison rises from his chair and crosses behind mine. His strong hands move my hair before going to work on the knot of tension between my shoulders. It feels way too good, and I swallow the groan.

"Am I the only person who's not worried about what we do next?" Ash tears into his sandwich, and a few crumbs fall to the floor.

Harrison's hands still on my shoulders. "If this conversation bores you, then you can leave."

"That's not what I meant. I'm worried about what *he'll* do next." Ash leans his elbows on the table, his jaw tightening. "If Interpol raided his club in London, even if they found nothing, you think he doesn't know? You think he's not pissed?"

Silence falls over the room.

Until a phone ringing makes us all jump.

Leni holds up a hand. "Right back. It's Debajo." She lifts the phone to her ear and heads for the living room.

Ash rises with his glass, bound for the kitchen.

A low whining from the floor has me looking under the table. Barney licks crumbs off his nose. His brown eyes shine with hope. I take a piece of meat off the platter, offering it to him.

"Sucker," Harrison murmurs so only I can hear.

My hand closes over his, my fingers stroking his palm as I tilt my head back to peer up at him behind me. "He's your dog."

Harrison's expression softens, his mouth curving up despite the weight of the day. He bends closer, his nose bumping my chin as he kisses me. My fingers thread into his hair, holding him to me when he starts to pull back, and I deepen the kiss.

Something shifted between us last night at the beach. He apologized for leaving, explained why he did, and I believe he wants to be better. I'm not throwing my heart in just yet, but for the first time in a long time, I have hope for us.

The coffee machine starts in the kitchen. "Anyone want..." Ash starts, but trails off when he spots us. "Yeah."

"Never kissed a woman upside down before," Harrison murmurs against my lips.

"Don't worry. You'll get better with practice." I move my hands down his shoulders, not letting him back off as I smirk.

Harrison's soft groan is tight.

A huff of breath and pressure on my thighs has

me looking down. Barney's planted his face between my legs, staring up.

Harrison chuckles. "I knew I was doomed the second my dog fell for you."

"Really? That was early days."

"You ruined my favorite jacket. I couldn't very well ignore you."

"You tried, though."

"Mmm. Hard to ignore a woman who takes center stage at your club and flips you off like it's her job."

He crosses the room away from me, and I twist in my seat to watch him. "Pretty sure it was in the contract."

He laughs. "I know we have a ways to go, but I will prove I'm the man you need. And I have something I hope you'll wear." He tosses me a secretive smile over his shoulder as he heads upstairs.

A dress?

A moment later, Harrison returns with a small box. He hands it to me, and I open the lid.

"My bracelet." I lift the cuff, my heart skipping. I'd left it with him before we parted ways. "You were keeping it for your next girlfriend?"

"I'm never buying jewelry for a woman who's not you again."

My chest tightens as I look at him.

"I haven't forgotten our date tonight. In fact, I've

got a private location at one of my favorite restaurants."

"Private because you want to eat me rather than the food?" I taunt lightly.

"Private because I want the world to fuck off while I focus everything I am on you."

He fastens the cuff around my wrist, but I can't look away from his face.

The ball of emotion in my throat threatens to overtake me.

"So, I'm going to have to babysit the manager tonight," Leni calls, rejoining us from the other room and pocketing her phone.

Ash returns from the kitchen, his coffee half-consumed, as if he's decided it's safe.

"Sebastian's probably right. Mischa will retaliate," Harrison says at last.

"And we don't know how," Ash presses.

The cuff glints against the black of my tattoo, its cool weight grounding me as I rise from my chair. "We can get through it together."

I say it firmly enough even I believe it.

18

RAE

*T*hat afternoon, I'm busy with work, but I take some time to go shopping.

When I show up for dinner, I'm feeling more relaxed despite the awful news this morning and the tense conversation at the villa after.

The restaurant is exclusive, and when I check in at the front, they immediately show me past the other patrons, up the stairs, and out to a lone table on the roof.

My breath catches. The scene is beautiful and romantic. Tiny fairy lights drape around the single slim railing that would keep patrons from falling off, if there was anyone up here but me.

Any man can be the grand-gesture type, but this is a precise gesture. A place that sets the stage for a meaningful conversation, not one so grand as to stifle it.

"Would señorita like a drink?"

"Thank you." I opt for a glass of wine to take the edge off.

I'm waiting a while, self-conscious in the silver dress I bought today that dips low in the back and ends partway down my thighs. Ash promised it was a ten when I sent him a picture, but now I smooth a hand down my straightened hair and hope Harrison likes what he sees.

I'm starting to get nervous when a throat clearing behind me makes me turn.

Harrison's there, tall and imposing in a dark suit, his shirt open at the collar.

His nostrils flare as he takes in my appearance, his gaze dragging down to my wedge sandals and back up over every curve to linger on my face. "You're stunning."

I blow out a breath. "And if you were any other guy, I'd say you took your time getting ready. But this is faster than pulling on a T-shirt."

He walks to me, tipping my chin up and brushing a soft kiss over my lips that leaves me tingling. "I thought about the T-shirt. I'm saving it for our anniversary."

My heart skips. "Our what?"

"Mhmm. Last year, you tried to paint a picture of what our future could be. I walked away." His expression clouds. "This time, I will make it up to you."

"With incentives?" I tease, off balance.

"Correct. This, in a way, is our one-year anniversary. On our second, I'll accompany you in a T-shirt—"

"That's not much of a promise."

"—to the Casino de Monte-Carlo in Monaco."

"They have a dress code."

"I'll break it."

I suck in a breath. That does sound promising.

He shows me to the table, holding my chair while I take a seat.

The waiter brings our menus, and I read down the list, freezing.

Sandwiches, like the one I made him on his mother's birthday after he got drunk the first night we bonded.

Tacos, like we had on the beach in LA.

Paella, like we made after I lost a gig.

"I can't believe you even remembered all of these."

He sets his menu on the table, staring calmly at me. "Raegan, I remember everything."

I've been the subject of Harrison's intention and intensity. He's seduced me with his will, but this is new.

Every piece of tonight, every look he gives me, feels as if it's without his typical agenda.

He's not beating at my walls. Instead, he's

wearing them down, like season after season of rain and erosion. Relentless. Unstoppable.

I want to let him in because I've never had anyone love me like he has.

I've also never had anyone hurt me like he has, and as much as I want to believe he's more committed to me than to his vengeance, a few gestures can't make me forget months of aching for him.

I opt for paella because it feels like a crime to order tacos or sandwiches at this great restaurant.

"So, what do you have planned for these other anniversaries?" I can't resist asking after the waiter takes our order.

"Not telling."

Impatience tugs at me. "Not even one?"

"No. But I have them planned for a good long time."

"Three years? Five?"

He shakes his head. "More. You'll have to stay with me to find out."

I'm stunned silent. We both know that's longer than I've stuck around anywhere.

"But we'll start small. Your birthday."

"I have birthday plans."

"As long as they include me."

I take a long drink, eyeing him over the rim.

"Relationship isn't all big gestures, Harrison. It's the day-to-day."

"Alright. Let's talk about today."

I stiffen, thinking he's going to segue into Mischa, but he surprises me.

"Sebastian told me about the man he's seeing."

"He did?"

His gaze narrows. "You knew?"

"He tells me lots of things."

Harrison frowns as if the idea of Ash is confiding in me disturbs him.

"He wants to be close to you."

"That's not why I'm bothered. It's because he's been able to contact you all year. He had this relationship with you I couldn't have."

"You could've," I point out. "It was your choice to leave."

"I thought it was for the best," he says softly.

Our dinner comes, and the conversation shifts back to Ash. Harrison tells stories about them growing up. It's clear he adored his little brother.

"We should've been closer after our parents' deaths, but he blamed me. I protected him from the worst of it. Ensured he had the best schooling. Kept him away from the media, the legal side of things."

I take another bite of delicious paella, feeling the night breeze whisper over my skin before I reach for my wine.

"Maybe you should've stayed with him instead of trying to bubble-wrap him," I murmur.

He flinches. "I thought I did the right thing. It

feels like the right thing is obvious, but when you look back, sometimes it seems there were only many wrong ones."

We sip in silence.

"I know you thought you were doing the right thing by leaving LA," I start when I set my glass down. "But it wasn't. Not because you left, but because you treated me like my opinion didn't matter." I lean forward, my cuff clinking against the table. "You called me your queen and then treated me like a pawn."

"I'm sorry I ever made you think that."

"Why is Mischa so set on chasing after you? You said you never considered working for his parents."

"I did one gig for them." My brows shoot up in surprise. "Then when I learned my parents weren't the people I thought, it reinforced that about me."

"You're a good man. Not because of what you've built. Because of what's in here." I reach over and tap his shirt under the edge of his jacket.

He presses my palm to his chest, and the steady thud of his heart beneath my hand is so warm and real it's a wonder I don't melt into him.

We finish our dinner, and he rises from his chair, motioning to me.

His hand on my back, he moves us to the ledge and leans both elbows over it to look out at the lights of the city, the black ocean beyond.

"Tourists come to Ibiza for the crowd. But when you lift your gaze past the party, we're surrounded by stillness. It's easy to forget there's a whole world out there."

"I'm sure your executive team in London reminds you that you have a business to run."

"It doesn't matter." He turns toward me. "When I'm with you, I feel that calm. I don't need to be on an island to feel it anymore."

My heart skips. "Where should we go? You might have an empire, but this girl needs to work."

He reaches for my hand, threads his fingers through mine. "Where would you like to work?"

Emotions collide in my chest. "I was working on some options back in the US." I feel him turn toward me. "I don't want to say it in case it doesn't work out. But the past couple of months, all I could think about is playing La Mer."

"You won't play La Mer." There's a finality to his words that would make me argue, but it's moot anyway.

"It might belong to Mischa, but it has nothing to do with him. It existed before him, and it will exist after." I shake my head. "I was still hoping he'd rethink it."

But when he hears I played Debajo, there's no way he will. He'll find out I'm with Harrison— assuming he doesn't know already...

"I'm sorry."

I cock my head. "You're not."

"I am because you want it, and I want you to have everything you want."

Damn, it sounds as if he means it. My fingers curl around his.

"After your final gig in Ibiza—at Bliss or some-where else—I'll take you somewhere scenic, and we'll laugh about this. But until then... dance with me."

He offers a hand as music starts from somewhere in the distance. Not club music, but strings.

"Ditch the jacket."

He obliges with a boyish grin, tossing it over the chair before pulling me close.

My lips brush his shirt.

"Since the first time I held you at La Mer, nothing has ever felt the same," he confesses. "When I set foot inside the warehouse in LA, I didn't picture you on stage. It was you dancing with me."

"My dancing is mostly hips. You probably know how to ballroom dance."

He shrugs a shoulder. "Only the basics. Waltz, foxtrot, rumba..."

"Of course you do," I murmur, laughing. "I tried to take a class at school. I could barely shuffle. But I'm done apologizing for it," I declare.

That's the biggest difference in the last year. No more pretending to be something I'm not.

Harrison brushes his lips across my temple, surprising me. "Good. Because I'd rather shuffle with you for the rest of my life than waltz with anyone else."

*B*liss is full, but I'm on edge, scanning the crowd as I mix.

I'm still thinking of my date with Harrison last night. Dinner was a dream. We went back to his villa and stayed up on the patio until the early hours of the morning, where he laid a blanket down on the grass and we talked and touched under the stars.

It's not as if everything is resolved between us, but he certainly wants to try. And he seems like a changed man.

Now, I'm back to the reality of playing the club where a woman died when it could have been prevented.

Which means there's something I need to do.

As I finish, I catch sight of the owner.

After a few selfies, I wave off the crowd of fans and cut straight for the bar. The bartender pours me a drink, and the owner nods at me. I lift my glass to him, taking a long drink. "A woman died outside. A customer from last week."

His eyes widen. "I don't know anything about that."

"You should. Mischa's drugs killed her. And you let him in."

His gaze cuts past my shoulder. When I follow the owner's eyes, a hulking security guard nods to me.

"Go with him," the owner says.

I stiffen. "Where?"

He doesn't answer.

The hairs on my neck lift in warning, but I want to know where this leads. Maybe he's decided he'll talk to me after all.

I follow the security guard, my hand tightening on my phone to signal my own security.

We're heading through the halls, and it's quieter after the door to the club closes behind us. When we reach another door—a VIP room I remember from my tour when I arrived—the security guard opens it and holds it wide. I have no choice but to step inside.

The room is the size of a hotel suite, velvet furniture and curtains. A booth is along the far end, a bar on the wall nearest, but it's the man at the center that draws all of my attention.

Mischa sprawls along the largest couch, wearing black trousers and a white shirt. His legs stretch in front of him, and there's a woman on either side of him. If they're not twins, they're doing a damned good impression. One is completely naked, the other topless. They're brunettes, unlike his fiancée.

Armed security watches from either corner of the room. They're not club guards either. These men look hard, and they don't move except for their eyes.

"Miss Madani." Mischa's lips curl.

My breath is shallow as I stop in front of the coffee table littered with pills and powder.

"If I'd known you were coming to my show, I would've played something for you."

"Believe me, I was more than affected." His eyes are blue, but gray-blue, like a dead sky.

I wonder what he sees. What he thinks about that makes him treat people like commodities.

"It's a great club," I say.

"That's why I'm buying it."

I whirl around to see the owner by the door. His face is downcast.

Mischa rises, ignoring the hands of the women trying to drag him back, and steps around the table.

"You've been moonlighting. At Harrison King's club no less."

Of course he knows about Debajo. It was all over social media, and though there are no new photos of us, there are conversations online speculating about Harrison and me getting back together.

If Mischa brought me here to hurt me, or to use

me against Harrison, I wish he'd get the hell on with it.

"He made me an offer. Besides, my contract isn't exclusive. I play where I want. If that means you're not interested anymore—"

"On the contrary. You were glowing. I can't imagine a single woman in that filthy basement didn't want to be you or that a single man didn't want to own you," the Russian says smoothly.

He stops inches away. Close enough I smell his cologne.

"Meaning what?" I force the words through my tight throat.

The first time I met him, he hit me. I have no doubt he'll do that again, or worse, if it suits him.

We're not in Harrison's club anymore. This isn't even neutral ground—security is his, and the man by the door won't stop Mischa from doing anything he wants.

He brushes my hair behind my shoulder. Every inch of me tenses when he leans in, but I refuse to tremble.

"You, my Little Queen, will play for me. La Mer," he whispers, and my head snaps up in shock. "One month from tonight."

HARRISON

There's a chance. Not a good one, but a sliver.

I've been reviewing documents for Kings—the ones I shelved months ago—to see if there's a hope of reviving it.

Because the fire marshal won't say for certain that I didn't set fire to the club myself, the latest reports suggest insurance will cover only a small portion of the damages. But I could leverage capital from other projects and put it back together.

It feels worth hoping for.

My date with Raegan only solidified my convictions.

Once, I wanted revenge. Now, I want it done with so I can have a future with her.

Which is why I've compiled all the intel I've gathered on Ivanov and sent it to the authorities, including the inside information I didn't trust them to use effectively.

I have enough resources to protect everyone I care about from Mischa until they figure out how to bring him down.

It's the early hours of the morning, and I'm finishing a drink when I hear the car I sent for Raegan pull up the driveway.

Barney lifts his head from where he's lying on the floor of my office. I rise from my chair and start for the door. When Raegan is around, I'm more eager than the damn dog.

She refused to have my security in her venue, so they waited outside, a call away.

I'm halfway down the hall when the villa door opens and she steps inside. My footsteps on the stairs have her looking up.

Her costume is intact, black leather shorts with a bodysuit beneath, showing off her long, curvy legs. The blond hair spills in waves over her shoulder, contrasting with her dark, lined eyes.

"You waited up," she murmurs, stepping out of her heeled sandals.

I cross the floor to her, and the knot in my chest eases with each step. "Barney wouldn't sleep until you returned," I say.

Her eyes search mine, relief filling them. "You raid Sebastian's closet?" she murmurs, taking in my appearance.

I'm barefoot in shorts and a polo, and I chuckle.

"Dry cleaning day," I contend, unable to resist reaching for her. My hands thread into her hair as I claim her full mouth.

Her hand finds my chest, pressing over my heart. She lets me part her lips with my tongue, moans when I take the kiss deeper.

I want everything deeper with her. I've always been the one to push, and she's been the one to hold me at a distance. But she's not holding me at a distance now. She grabs the back of my shirt, then strokes up my back. Her touch heats my skin instantly.

We're alone in this house. I want to fold her over the kitchen table, take her until she's gripping the sides and groaning into the wood. Then carry her upstairs and love her in my bed.

Before I can, she pries her lips from mine.

"What's wrong?" I demand.

Her eyes turn glassy, and alarm sets in my gut. "Mischa wants me to play La Mer."

I grip her arms, hard enough she flinches. *No.*

"He came to my show and—"

"He spoke to you. In person."

She nods.

My heart accelerates, a horrid thudding that sounds like my past and my future colliding.

If he laid a hand on her, I would drive to him this second and rip every limb from his body.

"Did he touch—"

"Just my hair. I wanted to get the owner to turn on Mischa. But we were too late, if we ever had a chance at all. He's selling." She takes a slow breath. "The only thing I could think is Mischa saw me play at Debajo, and rather than turning him off, it made him..."

"Angry?"

"I was going to say jealous."

Mischa pursued Eva because she was mine. Eva

was beautiful and ambitious, though I now see she was a glittering facsimile of a gem.

Raegan is a different kind of jewel. The real kind. The rare kind.

Mischa is ruthless and arrogant, but he's not stupid.

I knew he wanted to hurt Raegan in order to hurt me. But if there's a chance that's changed, and he wants her...

That's a million times more dangerous.

I reach for the pins holding her hair in place. "You told him no?"

I finish unpinning her hair and drop the blond wig on the table with the pile of pins. I want to burn the wig. If Mischa breathed on it, I want it gone.

I turn back to the woman I love. I thread my fingers into her thick, silky hair, spreading it over her shoulders.

Still, she doesn't answer.

The hairs on my arms lift. "Tell me you didn't say yes."

"This club is my dream."

I grab her arms hard enough she flinches. "He's doing it to fuck with me."

"Not everything is about you." The edge in her voice sets me back.

"This is," I insist, thinking of the boy who hated me in school, the one who failed to recruit me to his cause, the man who's never forgotten it. "You're not playing for him."

Her brows pull together, but she doesn't try to move away. "What happened to you not making unilateral decisions?"

My laugh is humorless. "You've got to be kidding. I assumed you'd see the reason in not playing for a madman. One who knows you're with me."

"It's the world's most famous club, Harrison. I'll be on stage. There's nowhere safer." Her chin juts out at me.

My abs clench, and the next breath I take is ragged. "I won't sit idly by and watch you risk yourself for your career," I whisper against her throat.

Raegan pulls back to look in my eyes. "You do it every day."

That's a low blow. A reminder there's a double standard.

But I inherited this rivalry—she didn't.

Last year, she was never in danger. Now, not only is she in Ibiza and playing for a monster, but he knows she's mine. And there's nothing the man lives for more than taking away what's mine.

Minutes ago, I was handing this off to law enforcement and looking at our future. But I need to finish this first, and our timeline just shortened. I won't let Rae play La Mer, not as long as that man owns it.

I can't change her mind. I see it in the tilt of her chin, the warning in her eyes.

She's the one forcing my hand.

Raegan starts to pull away, hurt. I don't let her.

I lean in and thread my fingers into her hair, pressing my lips to her forehead. After a beat, her arms go around me.

I breathe her in, my heart a thudding against my ribs.

I will end him. I swear to God.

"*F*lying solo again?"

Ash's comment has me looking up from where I'm working on the villa patio in a lounge chair.

I shift my legs to one side, and Ash drops onto the end.

"It's been a week." My fingers flex on my notebook, and I set it on the table next to the lounger. "Harrison barely eats. Toro won't say where they go. Natalia's worried."

Ash sighs, scratching his chin. "He's single-minded. Especially when he thinks you're being threatened. He's probably tearing his hair out at the thought of you playing La Mer."

"Harrison's turning into someone I barely know." I stroke the bangle on my wrist and stare at the crown beneath, emotions clashing in my chest.

I can't kick my excitement to play there. I've been thinking about my set every second. My publicist has been busy since I confirmed the offer, working with La Mer's team on graphics and promotions. I told Callie I'm about to play the biggest gig of my career, leaving out the part about Mischa.

I want the man to be brought to justice—more than ever after seeing that poor woman die.

But this performance isn't about Mischa. It's everything I've worked for, and I'm not going to let him ruin my chance to do what I love.

I'm over letting men with their own agendas shape my life.

"Harry's lost everyone who mattered to him," Ash says.

"He hasn't. You're here. Leni's here. Natalia and Toro and me." I shake my head. "Today he's in London doing God knows what. Secret meetings."

Ash cocks a brow. "You're not..." His gaze flicks to his brother's bedroom window. "If my brother's not delivering, the offer always stands."

His slow smile has me rolling my eyes.

"That's what Beck says. You're into girls too?"

Ash shifts off the chair. "Nah, not really. I dated a couple. But this boy in boarding school made it perfectly clear what I want."

"Dicks."

"So many dicks, Raegan." His blue eyes dance. "Do you know what you can do with a perfect dick?"

"I have a few ideas."

Last night, I stopped by Harrison's office after one in the morning.

I told him, "I'll be in bed if you want to join me."

His eyes swept over me, glassy and unfocused.

"If you don't, I'll take care of myself."

In my bedroom, I undressed, then waited ten minutes before I started going through with it, and I didn't hold back. Seconds after the first moan drifted from my lips, the door opened wide. He dragged off his shirt before kneeling between my thighs, yanking my ankles wide, and pinning me to the bed.

"Impatient woman," he murmured as his mouth lowered toward my hips.

Then all my words were gone as his tongue and lips wreaked sweet havoc on my body.

But immediately after we finished, he crept back down the hall to his office to wage war on a man who isn't under our roof but feels as if he's in every inch of our lives.

I force my attention back to Ash. "How's your guy?"

They've been staying together at the hotel.

Harrison's brother's smile is irrepressible. "He had a call with his lawyers yesterday. Said the arrangement's going well."

Gavin and the girl I met at the club event aren't married, but they have a child together. Ash said Gavin has told his girlfriend he's gay and that the relationship is over, but they're working through the logistics of custody and their belongings.

It must be difficult, but I still wish Ash had more to go on. I don't trust the guy after how he treated Ash before.

"Have you been in touch with the team?"

"Yeah. They want me to come back early next month to train." He frowns.

"Your contract's not at risk, right?"

"I'm secured another year. They can't turn me loose without cause. And missing a few too many penalty kicks doesn't count."

It still sounds like a lot of pressure on Ash. I feel for him.

"There's this place we're planning to go to tonight," he continues, leaning in. "Las Puertas Del Cielo. 'Heaven's Gate.' It's a lookout near Santa Inés."

"Sounds beautiful."

His smile fades a few watts. "We're not flying off to Hawaii to say I do. But it helps when the person you're into isn't living with someone else."

My chest tightens, and he kicks my shin lightly.

"Don't let my situation drag you down. Or yours. My gloomy brother isn't a reason to ruin a perfectly good day in Ibiza."

"You're right."

He grabs my arm and drags me toward the door. "Grab your bathing suit. We're going swimming at the hotel. We need to go somewhere to have fun."

After swimming at the hotel with Ash, I do feel better. I change and stop by a café in town before swinging by Debajo with treats for the staff.

"Dibs on that coffee," Leni says, swooping in to grab it when I carry the tray through the doors. "Thanks, Rae. Things have been rough."

"Because of Mischa?"

"Because of Harrison."

I set the rest of the treats on the bar, and the day staff descends on it.

Leni nods across the room, and I follow, folding my arms. She lowers her voice.

"This week, he bought more vodka than we would use in two months of high season so Mischa would run short. He paid staff not to work there. One of Ivanov's Paris clubs had to shut down temporarily, supposedly due to a rodent infestation."

"Harrison is personally sabotaging Mischa?" Things have escalated more than I expected. "Would that even put a dent in Ivanov's business?"

"Maybe. But more than that, he wants to force Mischa to fuck up and show his hand, ideally before your show." She sighs. "But in the meantime, he's causing more problems for Echo Entertainment than for Ivanov."

"He was in London today for meetings," I prod.

"Damage control because he forgot to sign a

lease renewal for one of his clubs, and Ivanov swooped in and made a better offer."

Shit. This has gone further than I realized. Harrison's taking his eye off his own business. He's been so caught up in sabotage he's hurt himself.

"Forgetting to renew the lease was a mistake," she says as if reading my thoughts, "but he's always known what's best."

I want to have the same faith as Leni that Harrison has things under control, but I can't. He's wielding his power recklessly, escalating what's between him and Mischa when I had hoped he would back down.

I squeeze my wrist, a habit, and glance down when I feel only skin and not the cool metal I've gotten used to again these past few weeks.

My bracelet.

I had it on earlier, but now, it's gone.

21

RAE

I'm still agitated from the conversation with Leni when I try calling Ash but get no answer.

So, I head directly to the hotel, speaking to the staff by the pool in case anyone found my bracelet.

No luck.

I head upstairs and quietly let myself into Ash's suite with the key he insisted I keep in case something came up.

There's no sign of the jewelry in the kitchen or living room or bathroom, the only spots I was in when I was here.

But something else is off.

Ash's door is open a crack, but there's no sound from within. Not even his light snoring. Alarm bells go off in my head.

I throw open the door of Ash's room, see his stuff

still there. No Ash. No Gavin. In fact, I don't see anything to indicate anyone other than Ash has been sleeping in this room.

But on the bedside table...

There's a collection of bags and pills.

No. Shit. Shit, shit. Has he been using the whole time?

I try Ash again. Still no answer.

Next, I hit a contact on speed dial.

"Harrison, it's me," I bite into the voicemail. "Ash is gone. Something's wrong."

I head downstairs and get into the car with my driver and security.

"Where to?" the driver asks.

That's when I realize I have no idea.

"Where would he go?" I mutter, thinking back to the room. There were no suitcases. No shoes belonging to anyone but Ash.

I know what happened. "Where is Heaven's Gate?"

"It's difficult to get to."

"I don't care. We're going."

⸻

When we arrive, the driver stays in the car while security accompanies me through the pine forest to the secluded lookout. Tripping over roots, I second-guess this idea more than once.

"Ash!" I call through the dense brush.

I curse as I scrape my knee. Once I emerge from the trees, I find a hunched form sitting near the edge of the lookout.

I wave off security, motioning for them to stay back.

My racing pulse steadies a few beats as I approach him.

"It's a hell of a view," I comment.

Ash turns. "That's why people come here. Americans. Brits. Everyone. They say they come for the party, but they come for this. To feel free."

He's high. Dangerously so.

I sit next to him. "Is that how you feel?"

His shoulders tighten. "Not so much, Raegan."

The heaviness in him breaks my heart. "He left, didn't he?"

There's no answer for a few minutes. All I hear are the waves far below, the insects in the forest.

"His girlfriend showed up. He left with her."

The raw anguish in his voice rips me up inside. Emotion rises up my throat, and I swallow it back down.

Ash inches closer to the edge, and I grab his arm. "Let's stay back."

"But you can see better the closer you are. It's like you could fly off into heaven."

"It's not so bad here. People love you and need you. The rest of your team. Me. Harry."

"He's here?" Ash turns quickly, as if hoping for his brother's presence.

"Not right now."

I wish he were here. For me, for his brother.

But he's in London. Not because of something important—because no matter what he promised me about focus on our future, his vendetta is once again taking priority.

"Come on," I say. "Let's go back to the villa."

After I get Ash to the car, I check my phone. Still nothing from Harrison.

I send off a text.

Rae: We need you at the villa. This is not a fucking drill.

HARRISON

"My hands are tied, Mr. King." The man across the conference table in the London boardroom taps a pen on the desk. "Ivanov offered us a better price, and the deal has been inked."

My efforts to interrupt Mischa's operations the

past few days have been mildly entertaining, if not even wholly satisfying. The rats in his Paris club were especially vindictive. But yesterday, my efforts caught up to me when I learned my real estate team was waiting on a signature to renew a major lease and couldn't reach me.

Because of it, I lost my lease on a fucking club.

Now I'm negotiating to ensure one of my more profitable venues—one of a handful of which I don't own outright—continues.

There's no way I'm giving it up.

I survey the executive at the property management company. He might be responsible for billions in real estate, but so am I.

"What if I tell you Ivanov won't be in any business in a few months?"

"Forgive me if that's hard to believe."

The windows in the historic building let in filtered light, and I shift out of my chair to cross to one, getting a view of the street below and the park on the far side.

"You don't have to believe it, but know this—it's easy for you to review paperwork and file deals and cut checks, but when you sign on to work with Ivanov, he's not interested in those things. He's a gravedigger."

"And he'll fall into one of his own graves by mistake?"

"No. The next one he digs could be yours."

Whatever he sees on my face has him blanching.

"Tell him," I start, "that you were mistaken about the dates on Echo's contract. The venue is no longer available. For your inconvenience, I'll ensure your son's tuition is covered at Eton next year."

He extends a hand and we shake.

I leave the boardroom grimly satisfied.

On impulse, I pick up my phone and leave a voicemail as I head down the hall.

"You can't beat me. Whatever you do, I will watch you. And cover you. I won't forget what you did."

I click off and take the three flights of stairs down to the main level.

It feels good to stretch my legs after a day of travel. The past week has been hell, but I'm on my way back to Ibiza, where I can hold Raegan in my arms.

The limo is waiting at the curb to take me to the airport. But before I shift inside, I pull up.

The rear tire is flat.

I knock on the driver's window and motion him over.

He rounds to my side, hand curling at his hip when he sees the damage.

"I'm so sorry, sir. I don't know what could've happened."

There's a slice as long as my thumb clean through the rubber. "I do."

It's twilight, and I need to get on a plane for

Spain, but while the driver promises to call me another car, I'm already tuned out.

Up the block, another black car is idling.

The back window is shaded, so I stare in the front for a second. Two.

I cross to the park on the other side of the street, sinking onto a stone bench with a view of pigeons playing in a fountain.

Less than a minute later, a man is out of the back and approaching me.

"I trust you heard I got the lease back," I say as he shifts onto the other end of the bench.

Mischa's mouth twists. "Never like to deal with landlords. Better to own property. Your parents always said that."

"Before you killed them."

He lifts a hand as if I'm the one being unreasonable. "I didn't kill them. They indulged."

"That's bullshit."

"Remember when we did that job together? We made a strong team." Mischa stretches his legs out, and it's like we're two old men reminiscing about good times.

If the good times were trafficking narcotics.

It was the first and last thing I did for his parents, back when he was trying to convince me to work for them.

"No. We were never a team. You never had a chance at recruiting me."

"That's what I told my parents." He sounds almost sad.

I don't know what they did to him for his failure.

I can't find it in me to care.

"Congratulations," I say, thinking of his engagement. "I'm sure you'll be very happy."

He grins. "I have plans for her. You won't miss her? I used to prefer blondes, but lately it's brunettes. Strange to have preferences change after decades."

My gut twists.

He's not talking about Eva. He's talking about Rae.

I lean across the bench, ignoring a pack of schoolchildren that runs past, and grab his collar. "You will never have her."

The children are barely past when two men—no, three—start to close in on us from around the park.

I didn't bring security to London, preferring to leave them with Raegan.

Now, I realize that was either wise or foolish as Mischa rises, dragging me with him. He produces a knife, holding it at my stomach, hidden from prying eyes by my jacket.

Despite the public setting, the blade is an unyielding promise against my abs.

Bloodshed is a crass way to get what you want. I prefer deals with wits and money. But adrenaline and rage pound in my veins.

"Coward's way out," I rasp. "You always took it, even in school."

"Would you do it?" He wraps my hand around his, flipping the knife so it's against his stomach. "You say you're not like me. Let's find out."

I could do it, could end this for all of us.

My phone jumps in my pocket. I ignore it, but he grins.

The next second, he's gone, turning and slipping into the stream of pedestrians along the sidewalk that borders the park.

I'm not a killer like he is. But I wish I were.

It's not until I'm in my new car and on the way to the airport that I check my phone.

A slew of messages and notifications fills the screen, and one in particular grabs my attention.

Rae: We need you at the villa. This is not a fucking drill.

I call her.

No answer.

I hang up and try again.

Midway back on my flight, she finally answers.

"What's wrong? Are you hurt? Did Ivanov—"

"It's your brother. He had a bad day, and he's really upset, and it messed with his head."

My eyes squeeze shut. "Thank fuck it's nothing serious. I'll be home in ninety minutes."

There's a long pause. "No. Not 'thank fuck,' Harrison." Her voice trembles, with sadness or rage —I can't tell which. "Not everything wrong in the world is caused by a single man."

She hangs up on me, and I'm left staring at the phone, frustrated and angry myself.

The plane lands, and I waste no time getting back to the house.

"Raegan!" I call when I barge in.

Leni's the one who appears, looking tired and wary. She tilts her head toward the patio.

I stalk through the house and find Sebastian lying on the table. Confusion grips me as I watch him point at the sky, stabbing his finger in the air as he murmurs words I can't hear.

Unreal. I hurried home with a gut full of panic only to find my own flesh and blood has indulged in some kind of party drug.

"What did he take?" I demand.

"Not sure. Rae found him. We're waiting for him to come down."

My jaw clenches. I cross to my brother and grab him by the shirt collar.

His glazed eyes find mine. "Harry—"

"Don't," I bite out, my grip tightening as I lift him to sitting.

Sebastian's hands close around my wrists, trying

to pry me off him.

"I've been trying to bring down the man responsible for all our problems, and you're getting high?"

"What the fuck are you doing?" Rae's voice at my back has me spinning.

"This is what you called me back for?" I demand. "My brother went on a trip?"

Her eyes flash. "You don't know what you're talking about."

"What I know is my brother fucked himself up. I don't tolerate drugs. It's the only thing I can't abide."

Rae grabs my wrist and stalks into the house. "He had a rough night," she says under her breath. "I went to find him."

"He doesn't need a keeper. He's an adult."

"And he fucked up, like we all do. That's why we have friends and family. You showed me that. How you take care of people. It's one of the things that made me love you."

"I'm too much of a damned bleeding heart, and it's going to stop."

Shock collides with hurt on her face. "I know you've been dealt some shitty hands in this life, but I won't watch you destroy your family"—her gaze cuts toward the patio, toward my brother—"or yourself."

Low laughter comes from Sebastian. It cuts off the second I level my gaze on him.

I nod to Rae. "Let's go upstairs."

But she steps back. "No." Disbelief slams into me as she tilts her head at my brother. "Come on, Ash."

"You're going with him?" I demand.

"He needs help. You have no idea what happened to him, and you don't want to. That's how I know this isn't you."

Her eyes shine with more emotions than I can name. If I weren't overtired and bewildered, I'd make her stay until I could tease them apart, have her explain each one to me until I understood.

She piles him into the car while I watch. I'm helpless and furious. A terrible fucking combination.

I call out to her, "You owe me a favor."

Rae freezes and turns. She crosses back to me. "What did you say?"

My heart starts beating again. I'm not sure when it stopped, except everything in me seems synced to her.

"When you first came here last year, we made a deal that included three favors," I go on, threading my hands into her hair. "You gave me two."

Her lips part. "Harrison..."

"Don't," I mutter, leaning in to press my lips to her hair as my fingers tangle in the strands. "Don't walk out on me."

She's not going to, I realize as she lets me hold her.

But when she pulls back, it's to brush her lips

over mine, cool and fleeting. "I am doing you a favor, but you have to see that."

Those are the last words before she disappears into the dark and I'm alone.

22

HARRISON

"*How* ow do you like it?" Sawyer drawls over the video call.

I tap the controls behind the bar to watch the thing skim along a ceiling track and descend down a column on the other side.

"The photographer bots are even bigger, sales-wise," he goes on.

I scan the club, empty except for a skeleton crew preparing for tonight's show.

Since Rae walked out on me last night, I've needed to prove I'm not coming unhinged. Which is why I'm at Debajo, running my business.

I hang up with Sawyer, and the robot comes down the track across the ceiling, bringing a Post-it note.

Apologize, it says.

"Don't tell me I hurt your feelings last night," I toss at my second-in-command as Leni rises from behind the bar.

"Hardly. Your brother and girlfriend on the other hand..." With a cloth, she wipes down the surface. "What's between you and your family is your business. But you can't afford to cut your own clubs off at the knees indefinitely."

The steel edge under Leni's voice makes me blink. She's always been a friend and an advisor. But right now, she doesn't get how close we are to blowing this all up.

The door opens, letting in heated conversation exchanged between security and someone outside.

"What is it?" Leni demands.

"Some guys out back in the parking lot thinking they can sell," security replies.

I stomp for the door, but the security guard clears his throat. "He's gone, Mr. King."

Lucky for him. God knows what I would've done in my current mood.

"Ivanov doesn't sell at Debajo again," I tell Leni. "If one of our patrons buys so much as a pill on my property, I swear to God I will fire everyone in that establishment. Do whatever it takes to stop it from happening."

She hesitates before nodding. "On it."

Two hours later, I'm back at the villa, cursing my brother and wondering whether Raegan's lying in bed without me, when the call comes in from Debajo security.

"Señor King, it's about Leni," the man says. "They were waiting for her. She tried to stop them..."

I'm in my Ferrari and tearing down the driveway. I don't look back to see if my personal security is following in their car.

The person who's stood by me for the last decade is bleeding on a table in the emergency room.

When I arrive at the hospital, I barge in the doors and demand to see her.

"She sustained multiple wounds. She's in surgery," a doctor informs me.

The blood drains from my head. "Call me the fucking second she's out," I command.

I head out the front doors, kicking a garbage bin on the way.

It's my fault Leni felt she needed to defend Debajo with the same fierceness I'd defend it with. To stop a deal in progress in the alley, not noticing she was outnumbered or thinking it might be a trap. But she's not me. And Debajo isn't hers.

An ambulance pulls up, so I round the corner of the building, more to avoid their eyes than to give them space. There's a garden, and I grab a tall plant with red flowers by the stalk. I tear it out of the soil.

Another.

"Señor—"

I whirl to face a janitor with his cart. Whatever he sees on my face has him backing down, hands lifting as he disappears toward the parking lot.

Sweat beads at my brow, my neck.

My jacket is the next victim. I drag it off, then throw it in the dirt.

My knees buckle as I brace against the side of the building.

I yank my phone out of my pocket and stare at a picture of the four of us at the villa. Leni, Ash, Raegan, and me. Plus Barney's head stuck between Rae's legs.

I've hurt them all by knowing them. They've all stood by me.

Until Raegan's words last night.

"I am doing you a favor."

In my quest to punish the man who caused me pain, I've punished everyone I love. I wanted to protect them, and I hurt them instead.

My eyes burn.

An object on the ground glints at my feet. I bend to pick it up.

My mother's ring.

I've been carrying it around. *Through everything.*

Those words inscribe themselves on my heart with a blade duller than the one Mischa used back in boarding school.

I thought I was doing the right thing. Maybe she did too. Maybe they both did. They thought they were doing right by Ash and me. By people who worked for them.

I need to fix this. If I lose everything I've built, every damn penny, I need to make it right.

I hope it's not too late.

I pull out my phone and type out a text because I can't speak.

Harrison: Leni's hurt. Someone attacked her outside Debajo. At the hospital now.

The ring back in my pocket, I stare at the photo once more. The woman I love looks at the camera with an amused smile. Before we took the picture, she asked if this was some kind of family portrait.

Leni said, "It's as close as we're going to get."

It is.

Once, I knew how to look after my own. Raegan was my most stubborn challenge—she wouldn't let me love her, wouldn't trust me or rely on me. Somehow, I was given the most exquisite fucking gift of being the man by her side while she figured that out.

Now, she's the person who called me out when I stopped being that man.

I've never prayed, but my gaze finds the sky.

Forget destruction. I need redemption.

I will do anything to make this right. Leni, Ash, Raegan. Everything.

23

RAE

I hated fighting with Harrison last night. But when his text comes through, the churning feeling in my gut is replaced with a block of ice.

I grab Ash and run downstairs and into the backseat of the car driven by security that stubbornly clung to me after I left the villa.

"Did he say what happened?" Ash demands as we lean forward, willing the driver to go faster.

"Nothing more than his text."

At the hospital, we leap out of the vehicle and bolt inside.

The woman at the nursing station tells us Leni's in the operating room.

"Did anyone come in with her?" I demand.

She gestures to the hall, where one of the security guards from Debajo paces, another slumped in a chair.

I race over to them, Ash at my heels. One of them says, "Mischa's men. She went out to chase them off."

My stomach drops, time stopping. "Where's Harrison?"

Right now, all that matters is he's alive. I'm terrified by the possibility that he was there too.

"I'm here."

The two words make me spin so fast I nearly trip.

Harrison King fills the hallway. His shirt is rumpled and stained, his hands covered in dirt.

My heart stops beating. I rush toward him, scanning the dark stains on his white shirt.

"I'm alright," he rasps. "This was intentional. They went after her as retaliation for my actions this week."

My fingers thread through his, and Harrison's expression fills with guilt and disgust as he stares at my clean hands and his dirty ones.

A doctor emerges from the double doors, stopping in front of us. "Are you her family?"

"Yes," Harrison says immediately.

The doctor eyes him up and down. "Husband? Brother—"

"We're everything she has."

The doctor relents, tucking a clipboard under his

arm. "She has suffered significant blood loss, but her condition is stable."

Next to me, Harrison exhales hard. "I want her transported to my villa as soon as it's safe for her to be transported."

"She should remain under observation for forty-eight hours. That requires staff, equipment—"

"Fine. I'll take it all. Spare no expense." He cuts a look toward the door, then back at me. "I don't want her alone here."

"We could have security stay—"

"No. It's not enough."

The grim look on his face makes me realize how agonizing this is for him. He's pale, his lips thinned, eyes haunted. He knows this is bad, and could've been worse.

"I want to see her." Harrison looks past the doctor toward the doors, seeming to think better of charging through without permission. "Can I?"

"In a few minutes. I'll show you to her recovery room."

It's midafternoon by the time Harrison sees Leni and makes arrangements to have her transported back to the villa later today.

Ash heads for the car, Harrison heading for his Ferrari.

I hold up a finger to tell my security to wait for me as I cross to Harrison.

"Should you drive?" I ask, leaning in the driver's window.

He lifts his gaze to mine. "Yes. I'm all right."

I nod, but before I can pull back, he lays his hand over mine. "Thank you. For being here."

I swallow hard. "Of course."

"No, not 'of course.' You've been keeping an eye on my family. All my family," he goes on, meaning Leni.

I pull my fingers away. "What can I say? They grew on me."

Our gazes hold as if neither of us wants to pull back from this shared connection. I'm not sure who needs it more.

Finally, I turn back and slide into the backseat of the car next to Ash.

This time when security asks where we're headed, I say, "The villa."

Ash cocks his head. "You want me to go another round with my brother?"

"You were barely conscious for the last one," I point out. "And yes, you're coming."

His normally dancing blue eyes are dull, but he squeezes my shoulder. "I've had worse."

We follow the Ferrari through the streets and up the driveway. When we get to the house, Ash tells me, "Think I'll go crash for a bit."

Harrison and I follow him inside, where a worried Barney greets us with a whimper. I scratch his head as Natalia emerges from the kitchen, looking equally concerned.

Harrison fills her in, and Natalia bustles off to get a room ready for Leni, and it's just the two of us.

His sharp jaw is as stubborn as ever, his mouth pressed in a firm line, but his square shoulders are slumped as he crosses to the kitchen for water, pouring me one too. I take it and sip, my gaze lingering on the streaks of dirt caked on Harrison's hands as he braces himself against the sink.

"Leni was always up for anything," he mutters, "including a bar fight. I didn't learn until later she was shy growing up. One of her friends from summer camp said she used to be timid. Wouldn't play in the dirt for fear of staining her clothes." His exhale is half laugh. "Can you believe it?"

I fold my arms across my chest. I want to go to him, but I can't. Not yet.

"I led her to this, Raegan," he whispers. "I blame my parents for what they did, but I'm no better."

The agony in his voice guts me.

"You can choose to be better," I say.

"My top employee is bleeding in the hospital. My brother is doing drugs from the same man who killed our parents. It's my fucking fault."

God, the blood and dirt on him is getting to me,

almost as much as the way he's speaking. "Come on."

He looks up in surprise as I take his hand. I lead him upstairs and down the hall into his bedroom, tugging the door closed behind us.

I pull him into the en suite. Then I reach for the buttons on his shirt.

His blue gaze searches mine, perplexed. "You don't have to—"

"Shut up."

I start running a bath and strip him down. He stops me only once—to set his phone on the counter, along with a gold ring that makes my breath catch.

I'm curious about it, but I don't ask as he steps into the bath.

When I start to scrub him clean, he stops me. "You don't need to take care of me."

"We all need taking care of sometimes. I learned that from you." I sneak a look at him as I wash his hands, the dirt under his nails.

He sinks back in the tub, watching me with half-lidded eyes. "I won't be responsible for any more people I care about being hurt."

"You'll stop going after Mischa, then? Because that's the price."

He studies me while I switch to the other hand.

"I can't succeed," he says. "Not if the people I love

are hurt in the process. Without them, I have nothing."

"Leni and Ash know they're important to you," I say softly.

His throat bobs. "Without *you*, I am nothing."

The painful balloon stretching my chest expands more. "It's not enough for you to put me on some pedestal I never asked for. To do reckless shit to protect me and anyone else. Any decisions we make, we make together. That's the deal."

I'm willing to put my heart on the line for him, but we can't be together unless he does this.

His mouth tips up at one corner. "You're right. That's how we'll do things."

A wave of emotion washes over me. "You mean it?"

His slow nod makes the block of ice in my stomach start to melt.

He stands and surveys me. A hard, dripping god in a rare moment of vulnerability.

"You're wet," I murmur.

He reaches an arm around my waist and tugs me toward him. I step over the edge of the bathtub, my bare foot finding grip on the bottom as the water rises to my calves.

"What are you doing?" I ask.

"I want you with me."

"I'm here."

"Not close enough."

Before I can decide whether to strip out of my clothes or try to coax him out of the bath, he tugs me down into the water. I'm soaked. My denim shorts are plastered to my hips, my tank top sticking to every inch of my breasts and heaving stomach. He strips the shirt over my head before getting to work on my shorts.

"Good luck getting them off."

"Challenge accepted." The glint in his eyes is the first hint of humor I've seen him show in a week, and I didn't realize I was starved for it until now.

He works the shorts off my hips, though I slide and send a sheet of water cascading over the side of the tub in the process. We're both breathless when he drags my hips to straddle his, the impressive erection pressing against my wet panties.

"I succeeded." The rumble of his voice strokes along my skin. "I'm claiming my prize."

The tension is as thick as the steam around us. I skim a finger across his muscled bicep, trace the scars on his chest.

"I don't have anything for a king," I murmur. "I can't sleep. I can't stay in one place. I'm just a girl from Orange County."

"Then I'll stay up with you all night. And in the morning, I'll follow you anywhere."

He crushes my lips to his, his grip on the back of

my neck desperate. As if he needs this to keep breathing.

In this moment, I need him too.

I know what it's like to lose him. This past week, I was losing him all over again before my eyes. I tried to keep doing my job, to appreciate everything I've built for myself, but nothing felt the same without having this man to talk to, to laugh with, even argue with.

"Make me yours," I murmur against his mouth.

His hands slick down my back to my hips. He grinds against the panel of my panties, where my wetness mingles with the bath.

Harrison's touch slips under my bra to squeeze my breast. I arch into the pressure, tortured by his rough palm and the pinch of his fingers on my pebbled nipple.

Every ridge and plane under my touch is perfect. I stroke down to brush his cock, the silky hardness of him. He catches my hand, forcing my exploratory touch to still. Then he threads his fingers through my hair.

The intensity on his face overwhelms me. Emotions so vivid I never thought I'd see them on this man.

Regret.

Devotion.

Love.

He drags my underwear to the side to position his cock. The first stroke makes me gasp. He fills me so tightly, rubbing against that magical place. I'm drenched.

My hips buck into his, seeking more friction. He grabs my waist and grinds in a slow circle. The intensity of his gaze makes my blood pound.

My hands slip as I try to grab the side of the bath. I fall forward, braced against his hard chest. My knees wedge themselves on either side of his torso, squeezing as he fills me with a long, deep thrust.

He's attuned to every breath, every twitch I make. All the emotions of the past week, the frustration and worry, evaporate in the steam. His humility is still there, but it's twined with determination. Conviction that he can give us both what we need.

We're making a mess of the bathroom.

I don't care.

I cup his face, soaking up his look of devotion before I kiss him hard. Harrison lets me take control of his lips, his tongue. Below, he's driving the rhythm of our coupling.

My knuckles dig into his shoulders as he fucks me, as I meet him stroke for stroke.

His hands knead my ass, building the pressure inside. His fingers drift between my cheeks, my breath hitches. When one presses behind where we're joined inside, I gasp into his mouth.

Nerve endings light up my entire body. It's surprisingly intense but feels so good. It's not something we've done before, but I can feel his need to assure himself I'm his, all of me.

"You okay?" he murmurs, pulling back to assess my reaction.

"Yeah." I'm breathless and dazed by the rush of sensation. "I want to know what this feels like."

Harrison rubs me in slow circles, a look of satisfaction and fascination on his face. The pleasure builds until I can't catch my breath, and when he adds more pressure, his finger slipping inside, I gasp against his lips.

I can't believe I'm allowing this. I can't believe I'm enjoying it.

He strokes my ass, adding a second finger which only makes me clench around him harder.

"Oh my God."

He slants his mouth over mine, curving his tongue to suit my silent demands. His hips roll, his hands knead, and the pressure within me builds. I sink my teeth into his lower lip, plundering his mouth, devouring him again and again.

His speed picks up, and I rock back, riding his cock and his fingers.

The eyes I love are so dark they're indigo, the sea on the blackest night. "Beautiful. My fucking beautiful queen."

His words, defiant and reverent, are more than I can take.

A shudder racks through me, lifting my body as I come. He tenses, staying inside me, catching me as I fall apart. He shudders again and I can feel his release, pulsing into me.

The tension deep in my core tears, sending ripples outward as I cry out.

A few strokes later, Harrison's jaw tightens. His gaze cuts between my face and where we're joined. The sight of him coming makes me want to come again too. He sees it and fucks me through it until I do.

After, he helps me out of the bath and dries both of us with huge, fluffy towels.

I'm wrapping a towel around me and knotting it at my breasts when he says, "You trusted me, and I let you down. I won't do it again."

I catch his eye in the mirror. "You will."

He stiffens.

"I want your word that we'll figure it out when you do." I collect my soaked clothes and hang them on the bathtub before starting out into his bedroom.

"Through everything," he says.

I glance over my shoulder and see him standing naked by the closet, turning over the ring in his fingers.

"This was my mother's," he says. "Found it in the

guest room with Ash the other day. She always wore it."

I take it from him, admire the inscription.

I wish I'd met them. No matter their flaws, they created something beautiful in this world—Harrison and his brother. Made two boys who turned into the kind of men any parents would be proud of.

"You can choose to believe in them," I say, passing the ring back. "It doesn't make you weak or wrong."

His throat bobs as he sets it on the vanity again with a nod.

Harrison reaches into his closet and riffles through dress shirts until he chooses a navy-blue one. Ever the discerning customer, even in his own collection. Instead of putting it on, he motions at me to turn.

I hold out my arms and he helps me into the shirt. The bottom reaches halfway to my knees, and I cock my head up at him. He fastens the buttons from the bottom up, deciding to leave the top two open.

The doorbell rings downstairs, and we both straighten.

I don't give a thought to what I'm wearing. Harrison tugs on pants and tucks his phone in his pocket before following me down the hall.

Ash sticks his head out of the guest room. "Did you hear something?"

"Probably the hospital staff bringing Leni's equipment," I suggest.

But as Harrison reaches for the door and pulls it wide, Ash and I flanking him, we realize our mistake.

It's not the hospital staff.

24

HARRISON

*O*f all the people I expect to visit me on a given day, Eva is the least likely.

Her blond hair is limp around her face. Makeup cakes her cheeks and forehead. Her aqua-blue jumpsuit is pressed, but her posture is cowed.

Her gaze darts past my shoulder. "Harrison. I need help."

I don't believe her for a second. "You made your allegiances perfectly clear."

"Let her in," Sebastian says.

I shut the door in her face before starting to tell my brother how stupid this idea is when Raegan cuts me off.

"I agree with Ash."

"You want Mischa's fiancée in my house?" Disbelief drips from every word.

Rae blinks at me. "I want to give a woman in obvious distress a chance to explain herself."

Fuck.

I jerk the door open. "If it were up to me, you'd be gone."

"Harrison King taking orders. That's a new one."

I pull the door shut behind me so it's the two of us on the step. "If you so much as look at Raegan, I'll have you delivered back to him with a full account of where you've been."

Fear flashes across her face, blinding and real, before she follows me inside.

Sebastian's sitting at the dining table, and Raegan's in the kitchen making tea. Still wearing my shirt.

Eva's gaze lingers on Raegan an extra beat before she remembers what I said and looks away.

Rae comes over with a teapot and cups, then pours into each cup.

Eva accepts the tea from Rae and takes a sip. Her engagement ring blinks in the light. "He's not the man I thought."

I cough. "Who did you think you were marrying? A saint?"

"No. But he was constant in one thing—wanting me. At least until recently." She sneaks another look at Rae.

I turn to my brother and Raegan. "Could you give us a moment?"

Rae finishes pouring tea and drops into a seat at the other end of the table. "No."

I swallow a groan. *Please*, I implore her silently.

A stubborn jerk of her chin. *Fuck no*.

Damn it. I called her a queen, and she is one now.

In full.

"He doesn't want me anymore. I called him out on it, and he got physical." Eva angles her head, and in the light, it's impossible not to see the shadow beneath her cheekbone. She turns her cup in her hands, lips pressing together. "At first, it was exciting. It felt as if he needed me in a way you never did."

When her gaze lands on me, I see accusation and sadness mixed together.

"You want protection," I guess.

"Why not go to the police?" Sebastian asks.

Eva's gaze narrows on Sebastian. "With the amount I've spent on skincare, I'd like to continue looking twenty-five for another few decades. Which is hard to do when you're dead."

"What are you offering?" I ask.

"Harrison..." Rae says. "This shouldn't be a negotiation."

I'm struck by the contrast between the two women.

Eva is willing to do anything to save her own skin.

Rae is pragmatic enough to know how the world

works but idealistic enough to try to make it better, even for people who don't deserve it.

"I'll tell you anything you want to know." Eva's voice trembles at the edges.

My phone buzzes in my pocket, and I pull it out.

Christian: Don't say I never gave you anything.

"Excuse me." I brush Rae's cheek with my knuckle on my way past her to the steps upstairs—a simple gesture to let her know I'm still here with her.

I hit the contact, and he answers on the second ring.

"This was you?" I demand as I reach for a shirt, shrugging into it.

"She didn't know where to go. I steered her your way."

I step out of my room, peering over the railing at the three of them seated at the table below.

"I don't want her," I say under my breath as I fasten the buttons on my shirt.

"A woman who knows Mischa's habits and secrets? You can't use that?"

A day ago, I would've cut off my own arm for this type of information. But I promised Raegan I'd let it go.

I hang up and walk down the stairs. At the

bottom, Rae rises from her chair and reads my expression. She jerks her head toward the kitchen and I follow.

When we're out of earshot, I explain about Christian's text. "Eva has enough information to take him down a dozen times over. But," I go on as she stiffens, "I promised you I wouldn't. That I'd lay it down. We can send her packing. Pretend this never happened."

Rae sighs. I wish I could hear the thoughts running through her head, could find out if they're the same as mine.

She's probably thinking it's not worth risking.

"One chance to hear her out," she says. "Whatever we learn goes to the police."

I nod, pressing my lips to her forehead. I would stay there forever if I could.

We make our way back out to the dining area, my hand laced with Raegan's. "I want everything."

Eva fidgets in her seat.

"Won't he know she's been here?" Sebastian asks.

"No. Because she's going back to him."

"Harrison..." Rae says.

Eva's expression fills with dread. "I can't."

"You will, or there's no deal." I can have her surveilled to ensure she's protected, though I'm not about to tell her now. "You won't tell him about our agreement because if he finds out you've been here, he'll end you."

RAE

Harrison's jaw hasn't unclenched for the last hour while Eva's discussed what she knows about Mischa's activities. Some of it we'd figured already—that he's running drugs through the clubs. That the money from that is bigger than the legitimate business.

"What about the bad drugs?" Harrison demands.

Eva picks at an invisible piece of lint on her jumpsuit. "I don't know anything about that. But I do know the cost of staying one step ahead of you is eating into his profit."

"You've seen the books?" Ash asks.

"I've seen his face. The one thing that pisses him off as much as losing is losing money." The room is quiet for a moment before Eva adds, "Something big is going down soon. I overheard him talking about next week on Sunday, but I could convince him we have plans that day and see if he'd move it to Saturday."

"Why Saturday?" Ash asks.

Eva's gaze settles on me.

"Absolutely fucking not." Harrison's voice is

commanding. "You are not encouraging him to do a deal while Raegan is in that venue."

"He'd be distracted," Eva says smoothly. "He likes you."

The way she says it leaves no question as to what he likes about me.

She wouldn't care if I was sacrificed in all this. Hell, she'd probably love it.

My hand finds Harrison's arm, the muscles corded and angry under my touch. "There's nowhere safer than the middle of the stage. He won't risk his business to catch you."

Harrison exhales slowly. "I want to know the layout of the club."

I push a tray of tea cookies Natalia must've left on the counter earlier toward Eva, and she balks. "I haven't eaten a carbohydrate in ten years."

I take two cookies and lay them on the table at opposite ends. "This is the stage. And this is the front door. The dance floor is here." I wave my hand over the space in the middle. "Where's Mischa's office?"

If Harrison's going to tell the police, it would help to have as much detail as possible.

Eva shifts forward and takes a wafer. "Here." She sets it down between the two cookies and off to the side. "There's a hallway here with offices and a couple meeting rooms, plus inventory to stock the bar." She takes another three cookies, turning toward the other side of the table. "This half is VIPs. They're serviced by their own bar."

"Is that where he does business?" I ask.

"No. He might entertain in a VIP, but everything is decided in his office."

"Are there any entrances near there? There must be one for inventory," Harrison says.

Eva considers. "Loading dock services the stock room."

Another cookie goes down, this one close to Mischa's office.

My heart thuds. "So, if the police can get in while he's doing that deal..."

"They can bring him down," Harrison says.

Eva takes another cookie, and we wait for her to place it.

"Well?" Harrison prods, clearly impatient.

Eva nibbles the corner. "Well, what?"

Harrison rises. "You need to go back to him before he suspects anything. We'll let you know when we need you."

"You still have my number?" she asks as she follows him.

"Someone will be in touch."

She flinches at the dismissal. It's deluded, but I feel for her, so I walk with them to the door.

"We didn't offer you ice," I realize when she turns outside on the landing.

"Oh. This is a day old." Her full lips press

together, blue eyes shifting over mine. "It wasn't an easy decision to come here."

I think of my decision to hide my assault, how some of the women my cousin helps with her charity are victims of assault by their partners. Eva isn't someone I'd empathize with, but seeing her like this, it's impossible not to.

She's halfway to her car when I chase after her, lowering my voice so only she can hear. "I know Harrison said we'd call you, but if you need help—"

"He loves you." Her voice is wistful. Then her eyes narrow, the faintest smirk marring her pretty features. "Good luck with that."

She might not betray Harrison, either out of loyalty or pragmatism.

But she'll fuck me over if she gets the chance.

"When were you going to tell me about La Mer?" Annie demands over Face-Time when I call her on the weekend. "You're playing the biggest club in the world, and I had to find out from social?!"

"It's been a crazy time."

My final show at Bliss last night was bittersweet.

I played some new stuff I've been working on, but with the shadow of what we're about to do hanging over my head, I couldn't relax into it.

"How are you and Harry?"

I think of the texts he sent me last night.

Harrison: Play me a song.

. . .

Rae: Something you can fuck your hand to later?

Harrison: Something I can fuck you to later.

"He's Harrison," I say at last.

"So, you're back together."

I roll my eyes. "It's a work in progress. Our relationship has some... extra pressure points."

"I'm glad you guys found each other. I had a hard time picturing the perfect guy for you. If I'm honest, I wouldn't have picked him."

"Smug, gorgeous, rich as sin with a reputation to match?"

"Yeah. But you're sarcastic, unselfconscious, and anti-materialistic. He's perfect for you."

Since I moved in, Harrison's been consolidating what we learned from Eva and communicating with the police. He's spent time down at the local station and on calls with Interpol.

Still, he's here, and he's more attentive than a week ago.

I haven't told him about the feeling I have about Eva. I'm not going to. I can't make him more concerned.

Though concerned Harrison isn't all bad.

Last night, he was tracing my palm with his thumb from the moment he picked me up in his car.

On the steps to the house, his hands were squeezing my ass.

By the time Ash shut the door to his room, Harrison had his hand up my dress and his hard mouth whispering filthy things in my ear.

He kept me up all night.

He's also bought me gifts. When I ordered a custom outfit for my gig at La Mer from a designer in Barcelona, Harrison swooped in and paid for it before I could.

He also found my bracelet under the bed.

What a fucking domestic thing.

I haven't taken it off since.

Even though there's a real chance something could go wrong at La Mer, I need to believe there's good on the other side.

"I'm ready for a vacation. It's mathematically impossible that one tiny person can create more havoc than an entire Broadway crew pulling eight shows a week, or an international rock tour hitting twenty countries, but she manages to do it." Annie's voice brings me back.

"You guys should get away somewhere while you have the time off. Get Beck to go with you. I'm sure he'd watch the baby. Or Jax and Haley." I think of her semiretired rock-star dad and coder-genius step-mom, their own kids about six and two.

"An A-list nanny," Annie muses, her smile

teasing and intrigued at once. "That's a good idea. Maybe I can talk Dad into it. He's been working on bringing Wicked back from the dead." The label he and Tyler bought as an investment last year wasn't only a business deal—it was personal. "He'd never say he's ready for a break, but when I talked to Haley the other night, she told me she caught him scribbling on organizational charts and muttering about restructuring. Of course, he's chewed his nails down to the nubs too."

I laugh, picturing the former biggest rock star in the world trying to do Harrison-like things. "Jax Jamieson's always going to crush the music part. Sounds like he needs help with the 'running the company' part."

"He does, though he won't admit it. And he doesn't trust anyone left over from the old management."

"He should call Harrison. Harrison might not have experience running a label, but he knows how to grow a company. And he definitely knows how to deal with the unexpected."

"That's a great idea. I'll tell Dad and Tyler. They might take him up on that. Anyway... What are you doing for this huge, career-capping show?"

I glance at my computer, anticipation surging through me. "I'm working on a few things."

I sound casual, but I've had ideas for this set for

years. A file on my computer. Things I swap out with new tracks from time to time. Thanks to that, preparing should be simple, but it's not.

I picture the open-air venue packed from wall to wall. The thrill of imagining it for years doesn't match the reality now that it's so close. I'm nervous, and it's not only about Mischa. It's about me.

I've worked toward this my entire life, and I want to do it justice.

"Go all out. Don't save anything for next time. I knew which show on Broadway would be my last before having this baby, and I'm grateful. Because if I hadn't..." She shakes her head.

"Take no prisoners," I murmur. "You're a really good friend. You and Beck both."

Her eyes widen. "Wow. Rae Madani going emo. There must be an apocalypse I don't know about."

I force a shrug. "Just the usual. Guys. Gigs. Grudges."

HARRISON

"You're not supposed to be here."

Leni looks up from a lounge chair locked into its

most upright position on the patio. She's wearing a pink robe that hides her bandages and holding a copy of *Little Women*. "It's been days. I'm supposed to sit around and get fat on Natalia's baking? My keeper let me out."

I picture the nurse in my hallway who gave me a frustrated look on my way out here.

"You need to heal."

"Fresh air. Look it up. I even grabbed some classic literature. I wanted something lowbrow but couldn't find anything in your office." She waves the book. "This Laurie dude has it going on. Loaded, big family house, bunch of girls who worship him... Speaking of healing," she goes on as I stop in front of the chair, "you cleared the air with your brother yet over the way you acted?"

I narrow my eyes at her. "We have more important things to deal with."

"Urgent, maybe. That's not the same thing."

I shove my hands in the pockets of my trousers. I haven't been wearing a jacket. The feeling of constriction in my chest is enough without the added weight of another layer of clothing.

Sebastian and I don't need a heart-to-heart. The few moments this summer when he's opened up were surprising.

Still, I feel shitty about what went down the night I returned from London. Probably because

Raegan planted this seed of an idea that I should've been here for him and I wasn't. And my damn brain weighs everything she says.

"Tell me about these urgent things." Leni's voice drags me back.

"They're above your pay grade. You're here to relax."

"Because some asshole stabbed me."

I shift onto the next chair. "We took Eva's evidence to law enforcement. They didn't want to disclose anything or budge on their own plans, but when they heard the detail we had from Eva, they realized this was a rare chance to capture him in a major deal."

I hope to God it protects Raegan rather than puts her in more danger. Because if this goes off the way it's supposed to, the police will be inside before a single one of Mischa's staff is tipped off.

"So, you put all your faith in the cops?" Leni cocks her head. "That's not the Harrison King I know."

I shake my head. "I'm trying to find a better way to monitor the situation. To have eyes not only on Raegan, but this deal." To make sure the two don't happen anywhere near one another.

I've been keeping my composure. In the moments it starts to waver, I remind myself that in a week, Mischa could be in custody and we could be free to live our own lives.

I've never wanted anything more. But I'm afraid to hope for it with everything hanging over our heads.

Raegan wants to go to London.

I'd take her to Machu Picchu if she wanted. Hike the damn jungle in boots and cargo shorts just to see her smirk. I'd suffer it all knowing at the end of the day she's mine.

Through everything.

"What about the robots?" Leni asks.

"The bartending robots Sawyer sent?" I frown. Maybe she hasn't been taking her medication. I should get the nurse...

"He has photographer robots," she says pointedly. "Ones you could station anywhere there are patrons, right? Plus Sawyer's company gets access to the data coming in. If the robots were installed at Mischa's club, Sawyer could theoretically see whatever they see and pass it on to law enforcement. But you can't order them for La Mer."

Leni shifts forward, wincing. She drops the book, her hand going to her stomach as she takes a few wheezing breaths.

"No." I retrieve the book from the patio, the wheels in my mind turning. "But I can order them for Debajo. Or be seen to be ordering them for Debajo. A lot of them."

"If Mischa finds out, he'll want them too," she finishes.

Yes. It's one thing I can do to take back some piece of control.

"This would need to happen fast."

Leni holds out a hand for the book. "I'll let you get at it, then."

*L*a Mer is shaking. The booth. The floor.

I'm in the middle of my set when a cracking sound from beneath makes me look down.

The stage is splitting between my feet, the gap widening with every thump of the bassline.

I drop to my knees and try to drag the halves back together with sweaty hands.

Instead, a piece of the stage falls into the chasm, and I fall with it.

Alice in Wonderland–style, I fall and fall.

Mischa's face appears, threatening, and he shoots out a hand to grip my throat. "I've got you."

I can't breathe.

"I've got you."

Before I pass out, the voice changes.

"Raegan. Love. I've got you."

I force myself back to consciousness. It's hard to breathe, but I focus every part of my attention on making my lungs expand, and reality comes rushing back.

When I blink my eyes open, Harrison's over me, expression alert and concerned. We're in his bedroom at the villa, light filtering in across the floor.

"Bad dream," he murmurs.

I exhale, wiping a hand over my sweaty forehead. "What makes you say that?"

The sheet is tangled in my legs, and he reaches down to unwrap me. Strong hands linger on my naked calves. In fact, I'm naked everywhere and so is he, but I can't shake the images behind my eyes.

"Everyone has nightmares before a big gig," I say, willing my heart to stop racing.

It doesn't have to be a sign of bad things to come. But the pit in my stomach disagrees.

Harrison tugs me into his lap, his hard body curving around mine. "My biggest regret today is that I can't watch you."

I wish he could watch me too. But he's staying somewhere he can keep an eye on all the happenings tonight, not only me.

"Someone will stream it on social."

"I can't get a personal reenactment?" A brow lifts, a smirk playing at his beautiful lips.

Insolent bastard.

"This is your problem. You've always thought you should get special treatment because you're Harrison fucking K—"

His head drops to my shoulder, running soft, devastating kisses down to my breasts. "Treat me however you want, Raegan." He looks up at me, and his expression steals my breath. "I'll come back for more."

When his mouth claims mine, I meet him.

It's urgent for reasons I don't want to name.

My hands stroke down his chest, linger on the scars covering his pec. It doesn't feel like a childhood prank. It's a warning. A promise that the man my lover calls his rival will stop at nothing to destroy him.

And after what Eva said... possibly me too.

If my dream comes true and I fall down a hole tonight—if the deal doesn't go down, or if Mischa learns we've helped the police—I could lose this man forever.

Harrison slips between my thighs, fills me with a familiar need I want to memorize. I'm torn between losing myself in this moment and imprinting it on my mind, my body, for fear it will never happen again.

When we separate after, my eyes drift closed. I feel him shift across the bed, reaching for pants.

"We need to get up." His lips tickle my ear.

"Mmmm."

He rubs my tattooed wrist, a habit that makes me smile. "When I met you, I tried to treat you like other women. I wanted to buy you gifts. I wanted to show you the world. But you don't like anything I buy—"

"I loved the yacht, mostly because it made you sick. Plus the headphones—"

"As for the world, you've already seen it." His touch skims up my palm.

"But I haven't seen it with you." My body is tingling from what we just did, and my heart is full of him. "I want to see where you grew up. Find a beach food truck on every continent and watch you eat from it like it's got a Michelin star."

"Hike in cargo shorts at Machu Picchu?" My breath hitches as I blink my eyes open. "Is that on the table?"

He chuckles. "I have a gift for you." He reaches for the bedside table and pulls out a box.

"More jewelry?"

I open it to find a tiny camera, smaller than my fingernail.

"So you can capture what it feels like to be up there tonight and relive it whenever you want. Because today is about you. And I won't let you forget it."

My eyes burn. I love that he sees me, that even if he doesn't agree with my choice to play, he'll support me anyway.

"It's going to work," I say. "Mischa ordered the robot cameras for La Mer."

A tight nod. "Sawyer will see what they see, and he's patched the police into the feed. I'm patched in too."

Of course he is.

He'll be watching the stage, but more than that, the hallways and any rooms with public access.

He can't see inside Mischa's office, but he wants to ensure I'm as far from harm as possible.

It hits me for the first time, the possibility that I've made this harder on him.

I shift onto my elbows, the sheet bunched over my breasts.

"Don't do anything crazy," I whisper, and his brows lift. "For me or anyone else. Whatever happens today, promise we'll still be here."

He presses his lips to my forehead before pulling away, fastening his pants as he heads for the door.

I spring out of bed. "I mean it. I can't lose you over this." My heart rate accelerates, and this time it has nothing to do with the nightmare.

Barney sneaks through the crack and accosts me, delighted to find me running and naked. I go back and grab the sheet off the bed, wrapping it around me as I dodge the dog in pursuit of his owner.

"Hey!" I grab Harrison's arm halfway down the hall.

His face is a mask of tension when he turns back.

"I'm not a good man," he murmurs. "But I will protect the people I love."

I run my fingers up his face, thumbs brushing the tight lines around his mouth.

I love you. I feel it in every inch of me, a raw, aching truth that's been part of me for longer than I knew.

God, if I lose him today...

I shift up on my toes and press my forehead to his. "Let's get out of here," I whisper. "Fuck all of this, Harrison. I don't need La Mer. Let's just leave."

His eyes crinkle at the corners. There's no blood-lust in them now. Only commitment. Responsibility. Devotion.

"There's a woman—a queen—and her stage is waiting."

He gently pushes my hands away, and when he starts down the stairs, I feel like the ground has split wide and I'm falling again.

My costume was intended to be daring.

A black silk tuxedo jacket, custom made for me by a designer in Barcelona. One side has gold threads woven through it. Underneath, I have black silk pants that hug my hips, gather around my ankles. The white vest, once it's fastened, dips low between my breasts.

At the moment, it's lower than intended. A button came off, and if I wear it like this, Harrison will start a riot.

I'm straddling a dining room chair and sewing the button back on, a needle in my teeth, when the tiny camera with a battery pack on the table catches my eye. Harrison suggested I stick it to my phone and set that somewhere on the desk in front of me when I mix.

But I can do better.

Five minutes later, I pull the last thread tight. The button is secured once more, the lens on the outside of my vest and the tiny battery secured with thread against the lining.

My phone rings.

Annie.

"Are you excited for your show?" she demands. My friend is a dark shadow, the sun at her back.

I take the needle from my mouth. "Excited doesn't begin to describe it," I admit.

There's a knock at the front door, and Natalia bustles toward it. She shoots me a frown on the way—she doesn't understand why I wouldn't let her fix the costume. To be honest, I needed to keep busy.

"We're about to find out."

I barely hear Annie's words over the phone because there's a squeal from the doorway and my phone at once.

"Fuck." I drop the vest, the button, and the phone.

"We came to see your show!" Annie cheers.

"Who's 'we'?"

Tyler's behind her with the baby. Plus Beck and Elle.

My shock and joy are overshadowed by dismay. Tonight, something thrilling is going down, but if we do our jobs, something dangerous will follow. "You guys can't be here."

"I get it, the club is sold out. I can get us in," Beck says, smirking.

"As usual, Hollywood misses the point."

I turn to see Ash jog down the stairs.

"Ash! Tell them they can't be here."

He cocks his head at me. "Well, they are." He cuts a look at my friends. "Quiz: What would stop you from seeing Raegan's show tonight? Warning from a mysterious oracle?"

Annie shakes her head, Elle snorts, Tyler frowns, and Beck lifts a brow.

"How about plague of locusts? Pestilence? Nothing?" Ash grins, grabbing my shoulder before I shove him off. "Sounds like they're staying."

*B*y the time I head to La Mer, I'm so amped up I could explode.

"Don't worry about us," Annie insists. "The nanny is looking after the baby here. We'll be over in a car closer to the start time of your show."

I hug each of my friends in turn.

Toro insists on driving me, and Harrison holds the back door.

"What are you doing?" I ask as he shifts inside.

"Going with you."

I'm grateful to have his presence.

We drive over in silence. There's so much to be said, but given the amount of our relationship devoted to banter and argument, the quiet is too precious to break.

When we arrive, Harrison kisses me hard. I don't

think he's going to let me go, but finally he pulls back.

"I've got your back. We all do," he murmurs against my lips.

I nod.

At the back entrance, I get out. My security followed us in another car, and they come with me.

I've always wanted to be here, and now I am. The club is huge and empty, but as we wind through the halls, it occurs to me that tonight it's mine.

Not Mischa's, not even Harrison's.

You can't buy a feeling. Can't own an emotion.

No matter what happens beyond the dance floor, I can give the people on it everything I am.

The prep is a blur. I catch Eva's eye once, in the hall outside the green room, but don't see Mischa.

I get on stage as the lighting tech cuts everything to black.

There's nothing but the energy of the crowd. A pulsing, throbbing beat.

It's my heart.

When I lift my headphones onto my ears, I focus on what I can do—my set.

From the first chords of my opening track of the night, the crowd erupts. The lights come up, and they see me and I see them.

This is what I wanted, and nothing can take tonight away from me.

It's my job to hold them in my hands. To take

them on a journey, to keep them safe and enter-
tained and away from whatever's going on behind
closed doors.

I lose myself.

It's the end of my set when my phone lights up.

**Harrison: There's a problem. The deal's supposed
to be going down, but the cameras haven't shown
Mischa setting foot near his office.**

Shit.

I scan the venue from my bird's-eye view on
stage. Nothing.

Rae: Maybe it's not happening tonight.

Harrison: She said it was.

"She" meaning Eva.

Did she cross us? I could see her fucking with
me, but not Harrison.

If she did...

My blood runs cold.

· · ·

Rae: He has to be around.

My set wraps up, and I head back to the green room, muttering to security about needing to unwind in private. Then I call a number.

A few minutes later, the blond woman slips into my room. I whirl to face her.

"You set us up. Where is he?" I demand.

Eva cuts a look down the hall. "VIP. The deal moved."

"The cameras didn't show him going in there."

"There's another entrance."

"Did you tell the police? Harrison?"

"No."

I hit Harrison's number.

"It's in the VIP room," I bite out when he answers.

He exhales tightly. "They won't move without visual confirmation of what's happening in there. Sawyer's cameras don't include the VIP."

This is bad. There's no way to get eyes into that room. If they don't act now, who knows when there will be another chance.

I press a hand to my stomach, sweat still sticking my clothes to my skin. My fingers brush the smooth buttons of my tailored vest. One is smooth. One has a slight bump.

I glance down at the camera. "Harrison? Did Sawyer get the feed from my show?"

"I'll check." Pause. "Yes. Why?"

I look at Eva. Her pretty face has healed from what Mischa did to it, but I can't forget how the bruises looked under her skin.

I know what it is to have someone take from me in a way that's unforgivable. To not only violate me but make me question myself. The doubt, the fear, the need to get out of my own skin because it doesn't feel safe.

This time, I know where the danger lies. And it's more imminent, more treacherous, than any I've walked into before.

But on the other side is safety for the people like the woman who died at Bliss, the ones who would be harmed by Mischa's empire. It's for the people I love, the ones who'd do anything for me.

I never used to believe in that kind of loyalty and devotion.

Now, I do. I'm not afraid of it.

The phone at my ear, I say to Eva, "Get me into the VIP room."

"I can get you in, but I can't get you out," Eva says.

I don't trust her for a second. But I trust the man on the other end of the phone. And my friends.

"Harrison..." I murmur into the microphone.

"Raegan, don't even fucking think about it." The panic in his voice makes me swallow hard.

"I need to tell you—"

"We have to go." Eva grabs the phone and clicks off.

As I follow Eva to the hall, blood pounding in my ears, all I can think is I hope he knows I love him.

28

RAE

*E*va's knock on the door of the VIP room is crisp. She's close enough her perfume hangs in the air. I breathe through my mouth and count the seconds, half hoping the door doesn't open.

I reach seven before the door swings wide, revealing a huge security guard with a tattooed face.

"I brought entertainment for my fiancé."

If Eva's nervous, she doesn't sound it. Her choice of words makes the hairs on my arms lift under the tuxedo jacket.

The guard's gaze rolls down my body. I fold my arms to hide the camera, and his attention stops on my breasts.

"Turn. Arms out," he states.

Shit. I'm really wishing my security hadn't been detained at the other end of this long hall at the insistence of Mischa's men that only Eva and I could pass.

I face away, my gaze locking with Eva's. Now she's nervous too.

He starts at my ankles, hands lingering on my calves, my thighs.

"Don't damage his property," Eva says lightly. "He'll be angry if you do."

"Hey!" The bark has the man freezing, casting a look over his shoulder. "Bring her here."

Security steps back to reveal four men—two guards and two seated men in suits.

Mischa Ivanov is impossible to miss even reclined on the couch. His suit is crisp, a red handkerchief sticking out of his breast pocket. Cold blue eyes see into me, through me. I feel for the camera, making sure it's still unblocked. Hopefully, it still works.

"You're excused," Mischa instructs his fiancée.

What? No.

Her presence might keep things from getting ugly.

But Eva doesn't protest, just nods without looking at me and closes the door silently behind her.

Didn't plan on being alone with the madman. Figured I could get in, provide Harrison and the police the visual confirmation they needed to take action.

Please take some damned action.

"Miss Madani," Mischa drawls, interrupting my thoughts. "I understand your set was tremendous."

"It was. I wanted to thank you for the opportunity."

He spreads his hands. "So, thank me."

I lift my chin. "I just did."

One of the guards, who is on his phone, hangs up and taps Mischa on the shoulder. "Third loading dock. In the kegs."

I straighten. That must be where they're moving the drugs.

Did my camera pick up the audio? It must have.

Mischa nods to the guard but speaks to me. "A woman who brings Harrison King to his knees. Perhaps I should be thanking you. He's been distracted enough I was able to sweep this place out from under him."

My heart kicks, the hard ball of tension in my stomach giving a degree.

"My empire is expanding," he goes on, and I can't resist taking a shot.

"Through cheap drugs that kill people?"

His smile freezes. "Every war has collateral damage, Miss Madani."

"You can't call it collateral damage when you're planning a delivery of the same drugs tonight."

Mischa's eyes flash. I've made a mistake. Maybe

he'll drag Eva back in here. Or he thinks I've figured this out on my own.

Armed police will be here any minute.

He shifts off the couch, adjusting his cuffs. "I can call it whatever the fuck I want. I'm more interested in talking about you. You are quite appealing, though you don't try to be. It's that attribute that makes you desirable."

Smug son of a bitch. I'm vulnerable here, but there's a part of me that won't be silenced. The assumption that women exist to attract men, that we're pawns to be desired and manipulated.

"I thought it was the fact that I'm with Harrison. I mean, that seems to be what gets you off. Going after what he has. His parents. His brother. His fiancée." I glance back at the door, toward wherever Eva's gone.

But instead of looking angry, Mischa laughs. "I've never seen him so captivated by someone. You gave him something his entire corporation never could."

"What's that?"

"Hope. And now we're going to take it away from him."

Sweat rolls between my shoulders.

Where are the police?

The truth washes over me in a sickening wave.

They're not coming.

Either they can't, or they're not seeing what's happening. If they could, they would've been here by now.

"What are you waiting for?" Mischa drawls. "You're a beautiful woman. Entertain us."

The guard behind me steps closer, and something hard bumps my lower back.

When cold metal slips under my jacket and presses against my skin, it's worse than my nightmare. At least if I fell forever, I wouldn't hit the ground.

Ivanov's cruel grin and the gun in my back say I'm about to do just that.

29

HARRISON

*F*rom the second Rae entered that VIP room, I've been ripped in two.

"Go in," I snap for the third time from the car outside, even though no one can hear me.

Watching her in that room with Ivanov, I'm dying a slow death. Sawyer got me a link to the feed when we figured out Rae's plan and patched it through to the police too.

It kills me the audio on her camera isn't working. I'll ream Sawyer out for this later, assuming there is a later for all of us.

If she gets hurt in there, I'll never forgive myself.

I should've stopped her. Should've taken her up on her suggestion this morning to walk away from all of it.

I rue the day I so much as uttered Ivanov's name in her presence because if I hadn't, we wouldn't be here. Now the woman I love is risking herself to bring him down.

The second the asshole gets off the couch and crosses to her, I'm cursing. Then the camera swings wildly before settling again at a new angle, one that shows a security guard but not her.

She took off the vest.

Or someone ripped it off her.

I'm out of the car.

A plainclothes officer emerges from an unmarked vehicle. "Mr. King, do not go in there."

I wrench away from him. "If you won't, I will."

I head inside, trying to wade through the crowd, but La Mer is packed. Raegan stirred them into a damned frenzy, and the afterparty is going strong.

This is taking too long.

I pick up my phone and hit a contact. Tyler answers over the din.

"I'm trying to get to Raegan," I holler. "I need crowd control. Everyone near the stage and out of the halls."

I don't want anyone in the way of what could happen.

He hangs up, and I think he's been cut off until the DJ changes to something else and I hear Tyler singing over it.

The crowd erupts, flooding the stage. A few people are in the halls still, and I shove past, reaching for my phone. I switch a few settings on it before sticking it upside down in my jacket pocket.

There's no sign of Raegan's security, or Mischa's.

But when I reach the VIP door, it's locked.

I throw my shoulder at it. Nothing.

A fire extinguisher is nearby, and I smash open the glass and retrieve it, then swing it at the door handle until it gives, and I fall inside. When I right myself and survey the scene, my stomach lurches.

Mischa is standing in front of the couch. Raegan's next to him in her trousers, heels, and a bra, her eyes wide.

Her jacket is gone, her white vest lying across the arm of the couch. Her headphones lie on the floor, the cord twisting along the carpet.

Rage and protectiveness unfurl from somewhere deep and dark in my gut.

"Are you all right?" I demand of Raegan.

She doesn't answer.

It could have been minutes at most since I left the car. I hate to think what he could've done in that time.

If he touched her…

I start to reach for her, but then I hear the click of a gun hammer behind me. The next second, my arms are caught behind my back, twisted painfully high.

Mischa grins. "You should've stayed with the Ivanov business. Your parents too. They might still be here. Loyalty is repaid. Those who work with us are compensated generously. It's everything we learned in business school, Harrison."

He's fucking nuts.

"I tried things your way," I say evenly, as if my heart isn't thudding against my ribs. "It wouldn't have worked out."

"You were too good for what I offered. Now, I have your attention."

Mischa crosses to me, flicking open a knife from his pocket.

He rips open my shirt, satisfaction glinting in his eyes as he sees the scar still there.

"I've been thinking about this for the past twenty years. This artwork is not nearly completed."

He doesn't want to kill me. He wants to fuck me up.

I tell myself that as the knife comes up, the blade hovering over my scar.

As it presses into my flesh, the searing pain making me bite down hard.

I don't have to look down to see blood trickle across my skin. I can feel it.

I can smell it.

"Stop!" Rae shouts.

Miraculously, Mischa does, turning to take her in.

Rae folds her arms. "Men are fickle. Five minutes ago, you wanted me."

What the fuck is she playing at?

I want to tell her to stop talking. Almost as much as I want to drag her behind me.

"It's true," Mischa purrs. "You have other redeeming qualities. Ones we'll get to once we've finished catching up."

She gestures to the other men. "This is some fucked-up boys' game, isn't it? Harrison rejected you twenty years ago, and you're still hurt over it. There're no drugs—you're just rich assholes fighting over your egos."

His face tics in irritation. "You're no queen. You're a child. And the deal going down in this building tonight is bigger than you can imagine."

He's supremely confident, and that's what she wants—to push him.

I inch toward her.

"Where are you going?" The guard twists my arm harder, stopping my progress and sending fiery pain from my shoulder socket down my spine.

I look down at my pocket. The phone is still there, mic tilted up. I pray to God the connection hasn't been severed.

Rae's lips curve. "What I imagine is that you're a scared boy who's ashamed he couldn't do what his parents wanted by recruiting one single employee." Dark brows draw together as she shifts onto the arm of the couch and crosses her legs. "And who had a weirdly personal thing for my boyfriend in high school—"

Mischa backhands her.

I wrench against the man holding me, the pain in my shoulder nothing compared to the panic in my chest. *No.*

Rae's facedown on the couch until he grabs her hair and drags her up.

"It's justice I want," Mischa spits in her face. "The pound of flesh I'm owed."

"You'll take it from me," I bark.

It's enough of an interruption that he turns slowly. "Or from her, while you watch."

Fear turns my gut into a block of ice before I can stop it. My breath is a shallow rasp echoing in my ears as I strain against my captor.

"On your knees." Mischa's words are for Raegan.

"Do you know how much these pants cost?" She's bluffing, but I can hear the edge of fear in her voice.

Because I know her.

And I love her.

"You won't be wearing them again," he promises. "You won't be wearing anything soon, and the only thing you'll care about is saying my name when I fucking tell you to. If I let you breathe long enough to say it."

He reaches for the buckle on his pants.

This room is squeezing the life out of me. I

barely hear the crackle in my pocket because I've been reduced to watching the woman I love face down a villain she never should have met.

Raegan backs away from him, realizing his intention.

But she collides with a security guard, who forces her forward again.

"My patience is wearing thin," Mischa gripes, turning to me. "You'll get on your knees, and you'll tell him to watch."

Ideas of good and bad blur together. Of justice and vindication.

I hate him. But what comes through that hate is something bigger.

Love.

I love her, and it's not about possession or control. It's about the way she teaches me to see the world. Revenge is worth nothing—there's no reason to fight for the past, but there's every reason to fight for the future.

I'm going to get us out of this.

I'll tear out of the security guard's grip, lunge for Mischa.

But the men with the guns will get to me first.

Don't care. I need to protect her.

"Harrison." Her voice is steady, and I can hate everything in this room except those three fucking syllables from her perfect lips.

She's held my gaze across a hundred rooms. I've

always felt the strength of that connection, even if she was fighting me.

I'm coming, I say. *I'm going to get us out of here.*

But Raegan's the one who opens her mouth and whispers, "Watch."

I can't make sense of the word until she shifts off the couch onto her knees.

No. No, this isn't happening.

With a chuckle, Mischa works the zipper on his pants. He's hard, and I want to throw up.

But her eyes are on me, and as I calculate my odds of kicking the guard behind me in the balls and making it out of here alive, her expression stops me.

I'm not watching. I'm listening.

Trust me.

We do this together.

It takes everything in me to stop fighting.

She reaches for his pants and drags them down to his ankles.

He grabs her hair, yanking her face back up to meet his gaze. "Faster."

"Since you asked nicely."

I hear something—the sound of voices in the hall.

Then the room erupts.

Rae's hands move fast, and Mischa bellows in pain. Blood streams from his thigh, where Raegan's buried the knife from his pocket.

I wrench out of the surprised guard's hold,

fighting the sickening pain in my shoulder, and lunge across the carpet.

I grab Mischa by the collar and hurl him toward the floor.

Mischa's head cracks against the side of the coffee table, but it's the gunfire behind me that splits the room.

I'm already diving to cover the woman kneeling on the floor.

*T*he noise is deafening.

Not like a high-decibel sound system, machines made to produce music. This is the sound of machines made to produce destruction.

I can't count the shots—five, at least. Some from the doorway and some from deeper in the room. Harrison grips my arms, covering every part of me with his body, pressing my cheek against the coarse carpet.

It's too loud one second, too quiet the next.

I sneak a look between Harrison's chin and shoulder and see men with badges and guns stream in.

They speak to one another in rapid-fire Spanish, and in my state, I only get one of every few words.

"We got the delivery," an officer says in English to

Harrison. "At the loading dock, hidden inside kegs of beer."

The weight on me lifts. I can breathe again, though my lungs are slow to expand.

Harrison shoves himself to standing and holds out a hand. I rise to shaky feet and turn in a circle.

One of the security guards is down. The other is on his knees, being handcuffed by a man with a badge and a gun.

The other officers stand over two crumpled forms.

The peek of a red handkerchief matching the blood seeping into the carpet is enough to confirm it's Mischa.

He's not moving. Neither of them are.

My hands are covered in blood. I should be horrified, but all I feel is a grim numbness.

"Are you all right?" The familiar voice makes me flinch. "Raegan..."

Hands grip my arms. Harrison looks as if he was the one shot. His brows are a tight line, blue eyes stormy as he searches my face. I wrap my arms around myself, fingers sliding on the sheen of cold sweat.

He slips off his jacket, wincing, and slings it around me. My gaze shifts back to the lifeless forms.

An officer appears next to us. "The camera was brave. Or stupid. We couldn't tell what was being said." He turns to Harrison. "Good thing you had your cell phone on you. Audio was muffled, but between that and the video, we had enough to move."

My gaze lifts to Harrison's, but the officer continues. "We're going to need statements from both of you. Ivanov might not be talking again, but based on what we got tonight, we should have enough evidence to implicate other senior people in his organization."

"We'll give statements at the station," Harrison says. The officer appears ready to argue, but Harrison continues. "We have some things to resolve first."

I head toward the door. In the hall, officers are directing upset patrons out of the venue. Fortunately, they seem in a hurry to leave.

"Raegan..." Harrison's voice at my back has me stiffening.

I don't want to talk right now. I can't.

"We need to find Tyler and Annie and Beck and Ash." I press through the thinning crowd, pulling out my phone and hitting a contact. Annie answers on the fourth ring.

"Where are you?" she shouts.

"Heading from the VIP rooms."

"Are you okay? We heard gunshots."

I cut a look over my shoulder to see Harrison's grim face. "We're not hurt." Because that's easier than telling her we're not okay. "Where are you?"

"Backstage."

"Wait, what?"

I'm pressed to the wall, moving in the opposite direction of traffic. I nearly get to one set of the double doors thrown wide to the open-air dance floor when a hand grabs my shoulder. I spin to find Eva, eyes wide.

"Where is he?" she asks.

"He's dead."

Her hands drop away. "Thank you." Her hand rests on her flat stomach, and a piece clicks into place.

She's pregnant.

I guess she decided enough was enough—if not for her, then for the family she could have. Her child doesn't need to follow in his father's footsteps.

The dance floor is wide open. It's easy to cross to the stage, and by the time I reach the halfway point, I can spot the figures on stage.

"Annie?" I call.

My friend waves. Her husband stands next to her.

"What happened?" I ask.

"Harrison wanted a distraction to keep the crowd on the dance floor." Elle drops off the stage. "So, Tyler took the mic to keep everyone here."

The numbness around my heart thaws a little.

"Beck said he'd steer everyone out of the hall.

Last I saw, there were dozens of people running his way. I haven't seen him since," Annie says.

Shit. The crowds tonight were thick. It's one thing to be on stage, but Beck alone, trying to get attention without security... It could have been dangerous.

I try calling Beck's number but get voicemail. I send off a text.

Rae: Are you okay? You went AWOL.

Dots appear.

Beck: I'm safe.

I heave a sigh of relief.

"Where's my brother?" Harrison demands.

We all look at one another.

Rae: Ash is missing.

Harrison grunts. "I'll call—"

I hold up a hand as dots appear again. The seconds tick by.

When the response comes, it's shorter than I expected.

Beck: He's here too.

My brows rise, but I show Harrison the message.

"You guys," Annie calls before I can decide how to respond. We all turn to find her holding up her phone. "I know it's been a long night, but before we leave... Group photo? I haven't gotten out in months."

31

HARRISON

*W*hen I woke yesterday morning, my chest was tight with dread and Raegan was in my arms.

Today, the dread is gone. But so is she.

I'm in the guest bedroom, and I roll to one side, exhaling hard as I hit my shoulder, which hurts like someone ripped it from its socket.

Last night comes back to me in a rush.

Our friends headed directly back to their hotel from La Mer, but Raegan and I were at the police station until after five.

We answered questions independently. Somewhere along the line, a medic put five stitches in the cut in my chest and reset the shoulder that had been dislocated before my dive across the room.

After the police released us, Raegan and I drove home in near silence. Raegan took a shower in the guest bathroom, and I washed off in the en suite. After, I padded out to the hall to see if she was still in the bathroom—only to see the guest bedroom door closed.

I opened the door to find her lying in bed, staring up at the ceiling. I crawled in next to her, pulling her body to mine.

She hasn't talked about what happened in that room. The way she kept her cool to gain the upper hand on Mischa in a way I couldn't have was amazing. It might've given me a heart attack, but I respect her even more than before.

But as I lay next to her, I wondered...

How sure was she that someone was coming? Did she think we'd left her?

I'm relieved Mischa is dead. But witnessing her at his mercy, knowing I won't forget it for a long fucking time, is a parting gift he would've appreciated.

The ache in my shoulder is nothing compared to how it felt to see her helpless in that room. That will linger on my soul.

Now, the door nudges wide.

I shift up on an elbow, hoping it's her, but the top of Barney's head and furry back appear as he pads to the bed. He noses at my hand and lifts hopeful eyes to my face.

Fuck, it's impossible to be a dick to a dog.

After stroking his head, I get up and pad out into the hall.

The shower's on—second one in twelve hours.

I want to talk to her, but accosting her while she scrubs extra blood from under her nails isn't the right time.

I head down the hall to my room for clean clothes. Barney follows, and after, we head downstairs together.

My brother is already drinking coffee and reading a newspaper.

"How was your evening?" I ask.

Ash frowns. "Uneventful. Boring even."

My brows lift.

"Relatively," he adds.

I take the paper from him.

He's not as pale as he was last week. Instead of being lethargic, his voice is light. His reactions are quick and irritated.

"I was a dick about you using," I say.

He shifts an arm over the back of the next chair. "Is this some kind of 'near death experience' remorse?"

I grimace. "It should've been me helping you. Not Leni or Raegan."

Sebastian studies me a long moment, then holds out a hand. "Don't worry about it. I want to get my shit together. I will," he vows.

I clasp his forearm.

"Brunch is at two down at the marina," he says. "Tyler and Annie are bringing the baby."

"Is Beck coming?" I ask.

An exasperated sigh. "How the fuck should I know?"

Natalia appears with a coffee, and I thank her as I drop into a chair. "Raegan's upset. What happened in that room... I don't blame her."

"What did happen?" Sebastian asks.

I don't want to talk it out, but I need to tell someone because it's burning a hole in my gut. So, I tell him everything, struggling to get through a few parts.

"That's intense." He blows out a breath.

"I wanted to save her." I pause, my coffee halfway to my lips, then set the cup back down. "It felt like I was the one on my knees."

Noises behind us have Ash looking over my shoulder. "Morning, sunshine."

I turn as Rae comes down the stairs wearing a T-shirt and denim shorts. I rise and hold a chair for her. She sinks into it.

"You were on fire last night," Ash comments. "Have you checked out social yet?"

"Been busy." But her lips twitch, and I'm grateful to my brother for reassuring me it's still possible for her to smile.

Natalia brings her coffee and biscotti, and Raegan murmurs her thanks. My gaze runs over the bruise on her cheek as she breaks off a piece of cookie and holds it out to Barney, who devours it and eyes her like she's the sun, moon, and stars.

Get in line.

Ash rises from his seat. "Brunch this afternoon. With everyone down by the port. If you're up to it." Her gaze flits to mine, then away again.

Raegan doesn't answer, and my brother shifts out of his seat and heads toward the door.

I can't stand the distance between us. But when I cover her hand with mine, she flinches.

"How's your shoulder?" she asks.

"It's nothing."

Not compared to what happened to her.

She looks away, and I grab her chair and drag it toward mine until she can't avoid my gaze.

"It hurts, love. Is that what you want to hear? It aches, but the only thing I cared about last night, the only thing I care about *now*, is you." I try to put my agony into words. "When I saw you in that room, I've never been so terrified in my life. I did everything I could to protect you. But underneath... I felt helpless. If he wasn't dead already, I'd have killed him for touching you. The second I got free." I grimace. "I didn't expect *you* to be the one to do something fucking crazy. It took everything in me to hold back."

Her gaze softens with compassion. "You waited?"

"You asked me to. And I told you, we're a team, love." I smooth back her hair from her face.

"You're brave and beautiful, and you came into my life like a storm and wouldn't leave. You taught me there's more to life than a list of assets bearing my name or a team of people in my employ.

"You reminded me that damaged people can still love. You tried to take down a Russian drug dealer. Unassisted. *Fuck*. If you need space after last night, I will give it to you. But I won't pretend I want to be anywhere other than where you are. I won't tell you I'm not jealous Barney got to lick your hand just now."

Her eyes glaze over, her lips parting. Every second she's silent leaves me ripped in two.

"You want to lick my hand?" she asks at last.

I exhale a half laugh. "I want to lick you everywhere." My heart hammers against my ribs. "How was it? Your set, I mean."

There's a spark behind her eyes, signs of life returning. "Incredible. The crowd was so into it. I felt like a priestess, Harrison. At the altar of the most awe-inspiring ceremony."

My chest tightens. "The way you wanted to play La Mer... That's how I want you. The way you felt on that stage... That's how I feel when I'm with you. You make me glad I'm alive, like there's some purpose outside of me. I don't want to live in a world where I don't get to feel that."

Her head lifts, and her dark gaze searches mine.

I can't dare to name the emotions there for fear I'm wrong.

"I love you too." She holds out a hand, and my heart kicks.

I grab her hand before she can think twice and press my lips to her palm. The feel of her, warm and real and here, soothes the ache in my gut.

That's not enough, so I cup her face and tug her toward me. When I crush her lips under mine, she meets me.

"Raegan," I murmur against her skin, unwilling to pull back. "I want to be with you. Tell me you want that, too."

Her phone rings and she yanks it out of her pocket. I want to hurl the thing across the room, but she looks torn. "I have to take this."

She's out of the room before I can respond.

***

RAE

Ash claims the back seat when Harrison drives us to brunch. It's our first time without security in weeks. Harrison's hand rests on my thigh, his fingers brushing the skin exposed by my shorts.

The phone call I took an hour ago echoes in my

head. I feel better than I did this morning, but the events of last night still weigh on me. My cheek hurts, and I resist the urge to brush it.

The way you felt on that stage... That's how I feel when I'm with you.

Harrison's words meant everything. I love him with parts of me I didn't know could love.

There's no chance of going halfway with Harrison King—not emotionally, anyway.

Since last night, my social media's blown up. But I don't know how to tell Harrison about the phone call I got earlier.

Harrison finds parking, and we get out at the port. The restaurant is open air, with jaunty blue-and-white-striped umbrellas mimicking the sea. Our friends are already at a table, and my chest expands.

The last time I went through hell, I was alone.

I'm not anymore.

"Good morning, superstar." Annie passes the baby to Tyler so she can rise and hug me. "Or should I say afternoon?"

"Late night," I say as Harrison pulls out my chair and claims one on the other side.

"About that..." Tyler starts, and I stiffen. I don't want to rehash it again.

Beck leans in. "Yeah. Let's hear it." He looks around the table. "How'd the set feel?"

The knot in my chest loosens. "Amazing. I have a

dozen messages from my publicist I haven't returned with requests for interviews, even a documentary."

"That's so great!" Annie gushes, and even Elle bobs her head.

Beck snorts. "And you didn't want to be on my TV show."

"I didn't say yes to the documentary." I sneak a look at Harrison.

Because there might be something bigger.

The waitress comes to get our drink order.

"What's next for everyone?" Elle asks, looking around the circle of us. "We brought down Harrison's nemesis, right?"

Tyler nods. "Paid you back for saving my life."

"You never told me what happened," Annie prods.

Harrison and Tyler exchange a look before Tyler says, "I was driving in London. Wrong side of the road. I got messed up and drove into a fountain."

"You're joking. I pictured it as something crazy or sexy or dramatic," Annie says.

"It was dramatic," Harrison weighs in. "The man drove into a stone angel. Water was spurting from her navel."

Tyler winces. "It wasn't pretty."

"You should save that kind of drama for my show," Beck goads.

"I'm not going on your show."

Beck shifts an arm over the back of Tyler's seat.

"It's one of the top ten streaming shows, and we're only in the first season."

"People are bored and stupid if they want to watch you fuck around," Ash drawls.

"My fucking around," Beck says, "is charming."

The baby fusses, and Beck motions to Tyler, who passes her over.

Within moments, Rose quiets.

"What about you?" Annie asks Harrison.

"It'll take time for Mischa's estate to be worked out, but as the investigation unfolds, many of his assets will be repossessed and sold off. I'll be first in line." His gaze meets mine.

I squeeze his hand. He's always wanted that club, and I can't expect that to change now.

More than that, I want him to have it.

"You could be back playing there sooner than you think," he murmurs.

I shift in my chair. "I got a call this morning from DJ Maxx. This guy I used to work with. I never liked him, but he's put in a word for me about a residency in Vegas."

Everyone gasps and gushes, but Harrison goes still next to me.

"When would this residency commence?" he murmurs when the waitress brings our drinks.

"Four months." He doesn't answer, so I add, "I've been traveling forever. Maybe it's time to put down roots. I want more than living out of a suitcase. I could buy a place. Hell, I could be a grownup. Even get my own espresso maker." I try to joke, but he doesn't smile.

"An espresso maker in Vegas."

I lift a shoulder.

I can picture it. Crowds there to see me, a club to call my own. The familiarity was one of the things I loved about Debajo, but I've outgrown it. I want a new challenge.

But I don't want it without him.

Harrison's hand resting on my knee withdraws. His ocean-blue eyes I love cloud, and he rises abruptly from his seat, tossing his napkin on the table before addressing the table. "Excuse me. I'm afraid I can't stay."

Before I can say a word, he's halfway to his car.

32

RAE

"*H*arrison?" I call into the house.

There's no answer, but Barney peers through the railing upstairs.

I hung out with my friends over lunch before they had to fly back, pretending the man I love more than anything didn't walk out on us and take my heart with him.

When I return to the villa, I'm resolved.

I want Harrison. The rest we'll figure out.

I step out of my sandals and head across the room, taking the stairs in bare feet. I pause at the top.

There's movement in Harrison's room, a shadow falling across the open doorway.

"I know I sprung the Vegas thing on you, but I want a future. And I want it with..."

When I step inside, he's waiting.

My attention drifts to the matching set of Louis Vuitton luggage on the bed. I reach for one and open it, finding it full of my belongings. "What is this?"

"Proper bags. For more than a handful of items. You said you wanted to settle down. Doesn't mean you won't travel occasionally, but this will get you started."

His thoughtfulness slices through the knot in my stomach.

"This is a lot of luggage. What could possibly be in..." I unzip the second bag, and the silver appliance glints up at me. "The espresso machine?" My jaw drops.

"I bought it for you," he murmurs from behind me.

"You're insane."

"Only since I met you. You're impossible to please."

"That's because there's nothing you could give me that would make me happy."

Because what I want is you.

He frowns, nodding to the next suitcase. "Look anyway."

I roll my eyes but open the top.

The contents have my hand dropping to my side.

Rows of folded, pressed dress shirts stare up at me. Neatly looped belts. Folded slacks.

The window is open, but there's not enough air

in the room. My throat works for a moment before I can make a sound.

"Your things?" I force my gaze to meet his, and when I do, it's full of so much emotion I'm tingling everywhere.

"Consider me newly acquired baggage. I love you. You're not going anywhere without me."

Hope surges through me. I want to so badly. I know he usually leaves Ibiza at the end of the season, but for London. The last time he was in the US, it was for Kings, which is a pile of rubble. I can't quite believe this man would drop everything to follow me.

"Even Vegas?"

He nods. "I made a call. We have a penthouse at the Wynn."

My slow smile won't stop. "God, you're arrogant. I haven't even invited you."

Harrison drags me against him, his hard body warm through our clothes. "You owe me one favor—"

"Keep it," I interrupt, breathless. "This time, you're doing me one."

His eyes warm with love and desire, and he drags me up to his lips. My hands fall to his chest as he kisses me. In this moment, I have everything—a home, a family, someone I adore who loves me back, when I want him to and when I don't.

"What will you even do in Vegas?" I pant, pulling away an inch.

He brushes his thumb across my lips. "It's close to LA. I can run my business from there."

"And La Mer?"

He shrugs. "I'll put in an offer when it comes up. Leni would love to take it on and find the right person to run it."

I shake my head, disbelieving. "I can't believe this."

"Worked out well for me too." His quick grin is sexy as hell. "This way, you still owe me a favor."

"There's an expiry date on those."

"No such thing."

Harrison lifts me into his arms, and my legs go around him.

He tastes like sun and sand and man, and when he claims my mouth, my arms wind around his neck without permission.

I kiss him back, with relief and love and the kind of hope I never thought I'd feel.

Barney barks, and we reluctantly part. I frown, reaching for his collar. It matches the luggage.

"Barney's coming?" I demand.

"Charter leaves tomorrow. If you'd rather avoid a man you hate, you can fly commercial."

I grin. "How terrible."

He kisses me again, pushing me back toward the bed, and we find a spot between the luggage. I kick at one of the bags, and there's a loud bang as it crashes to the floor.

The espresso maker.

I look guiltily up at Harrison.

"Oh, you're in trouble now," he murmurs before his mouth descends.

EPILOGUE

RAE

Six months later

The crowd is amazing.

From my raised platform, I get a look over the top of the dance floor to the booths circling the floor at the Vegas club.

In the two months since my residency started, each time I take the stage, my mind is blown again.

Still, tonight is special.

I take a sip of the vodka soda in front of me, the buzz going to my head. I spent my life keeping secrets, but suddenly I have news, and I can't wait to share it.

The nearest booth is occupied by half a dozen execs in suits with Harrison in the center.

I take advantage of my angle and drink him in. His sharp jaw and nose, firm mouth, muscled shoulders and chest beneath the custom suit.

I send a text quickly after a transition.

Rae: Charm them yet?

He glances at his phone, typing with a smirk.

Harrison: That's your job.

He shoots me a hot look and pockets the device before returning to his conversation.

This isn't his club, but he came to see me, and brought some prospective partners to discuss collaborating on a new project. While he didn't give me all the details, I'm praying it works out.

Harrison likes Vegas. It suits him, its flash and flair with an edge beneath the surface.

He has zero problem getting businesspeople to come here to see him, and I've been pleasantly surprised how little he's traveled since we arrived here.

I don't hate it either.

While we spend most of our time living at our penthouse at the Wynn, we do days off in LA and we've been to London twice to see Ash.

The only wrinkle is that a top DJ is normally travelling two hundred nights a year or more, something we knew we'd have to take a hard look at once my residency was up.

I can tell Harrison would rather stay put. But it hasn't been clear how long we can make that work.

I refocus on my set, and the crowd is lost in the music, in me.

At one point, I see the execs shake hands like they've done a deal.

I dash off a text.

Rae: Looks like my magic worked.

This time, Harrison looks my way in an instant. His expression, full of love and admiration, steals my breath.

He lifts a hand, and I think he's going to flip me off. My heart kicks as I think of our old Ibiza tradition.

Instead, he blows me an air kiss.

Fuck me.

I'm grinning like a moron, and I don't even care.

His gaze stripped me bare when I dressed for tonight, my mermaid-inspired getup an homage to the water-themed club, with a cropped, lilac lace top that leaves my navel exposed and green pants that hug my hips and butt.

My body tingles with anticipation because after my set, I have more to go home to than a hot bath and a sleepless night.

I have a man who loves me.

Two years ago, all I wanted was to play La Mer, but I didn't realize who I'd become in making that dream come true.

Now, I'm in love with the man who owns it.

A trustee in charge of Mischa's business assets until Eva's unborn child can inherit decided La Mer was too huge to run effectively and should be sold to an attractive buyer.

Good thing an attractive buyer was available.

Very attractive, if I may say so. But I'm biased because every night, he wraps those very attractive arms around me.

I wrap my set to screams and applause and head out of the booth. After, I'm lingering with fans to take selfies when my phone buzzes.

Harrison: Come find me.

. . .

I shake my head, typing back with a grin.

Rae: A little busy. Why don't you come find me?

A few moments later, there's a response.

Harrison: Because if I come find you, I'll drag you into the nearest corner and fuck you senseless. I don't care who's watching.

I'm already damp with sweat, but now my panties are sticking even more.

When I'm good and ready, I weave my way toward his booth.

As if he feels my presence, he turns and reaches for my hand.

"Gentlemen," he says. "This is Raegan Madani. My..."

He trails off, and I look up, arching a brow.

He typically introduces me as his girlfriend. Though we think of ourselves as partners, it's a possessive thing for him, and I don't hate it.

But now, he doesn't say anything.

I'm spared overthinking it when men whisper-shout compliments on the show.

A booth girl shows up and begins pouring Dom, handing out glasses starting with me.

"Raegan"—Harrison takes his own glass and lifts it—"these gentlemen have agreed to invest in an expansion of Echo Entertainment in America." He pauses, and I see the emotion behind his eyes. "We're going to rebuild Kings."

My heart kicks hard in my chest as he clinks his glass to mine.

I ignore the champagne and press up on my toes to kiss him hard. "Hell yes," I tell him with a grin.

When he tugs me against his side, stroking a hand down my back to my ass where they can't see, my happiness is overtaken by a sudden jolt of arousal.

"Perhaps we can talk her into an exclusive partnership next year," another man suggests.

I raise a brow. "Unfortunately, that's going to be impossible."

Harrison's hand on my ass stills. While I like playing for him once in a while, we've learned it's best if I keep my work separate, but he's noticed my firm words. "Why is that?"

I think of the news that's been bubbling in my chest all night.

"Because I've committed to playing here for another six months."

Harrison's mouth parts in surprise. "Since fucking when?"

I bite my cheek. "This afternoon. I had a meeting with the owner, and we discussed it."

Six months in one place. The penthouse Harrison found personally. Our luggage stored in the closet, Barney lounging on the carpet.

I can't tell if he's upset I didn't let him in on it or simply stunned. At least not until he threads a hand into my hair and jerks me toward him, taking the kiss I planted on him before and raising it to straight-up tongue-fucking, audience or no.

The fact that I matter more to him than work makes me move into his lips, the invitation of his body, the way his arms drag me closer.

When we come up for air, he's only looking at me.

"I didn't mean to interrupt your business," I pant, innocent. I flick a glance to the men who've started talking amongst themselves given the awkwardness.

Harrison's eyes flash. "Business is over. I'm taking you home."

"You want to wrestle for the good side of the bed?"

Harrison leans in to whisper against my ear. "You can have it. After I fuck you in it until you're too sore to move."

HARRISON

When we get back to our penthouse at the Wynn, Barney's passed out on the carpet. He lifts his head as we enter, ears twitching while Raegan sets her bag on a hook, then flops back down.

"I'd say he's adjusted rather well," I comment, stretching my neck.

Rae steps out of her heels, groaning a little when her feet hit the carpet. "Why not? It feels like home."

Some days I can't believe she's here—in front of me, beside me, under me. She is every bit the queen I never knew I wanted.

No, needed.

I shrug out of my jacket and toss it on the hall table without looking.

"When were you going to tell me you decided you wanted to stay?" I ask.

We'd talked about it as a possibility, but I didn't want to pressure her. While we're becoming more comfortable together with our routines as a couple, her career means being available to play to crowds all over the world.

It's part of the job, and part of the thrill.

"Just recently. Everything I want is here."

This is good news. I drag her against me. "Dinner at Picasso?" I think of the restaurant at the Bellagio.

"And shopping," she deadpans breathily against my lips.

"But mostly..."

"...Barney," she says.

The dog perks up once again.

For that, I toss her over my shoulder. "You're in trouble."

"Put me down! Being British doesn't make this any less caveman."

"No, but it means I can stare down my nose at you imperiously when I decide to drop you."

I flick the lights by the door with my free hand, and the soft glow from behind the dark wood headboard brings our bedroom into focus.

I toss Raegan on the bed, taking a moment to appreciate the view from here.

Her costume is sexy, a joke and a provocation at once, like only the woman I love can pull off. Her curves are decadent, but it's the confidence beneath, the ownership of who she is, that's most attractive.

"This outfit is ridiculous," I rasp.

Rae angles her chin up, offering me full lips and knowing eyes in the semidarkness. "And here I figured you'd like it. Seeing as how you're the clothes whore."

I'm already hard in my pants.

I take my time stripping her out of her obscenely sexy costume and tossing it on the floor.

The lingerie beneath is lace, matching the color

of her skin. As I shift over her, I imagine it darkening when it's wet from my tongue, her slickness.

Her fingers thread through mine, and I drag her hands over her head, pinning them against the headboard.

"Save your breath, love," I murmur. "The only thing you'll be calling me in a moment is a god."

She grins, and I go to work making it so.

I touch every curve, following my hands with my mouth, until she's moaning and incoherent. Then she helps strip my shirt and trousers off, and when I turn her over and yank up her hips to slip inside her bare, my gaze locks on the floor-to-ceiling mirror across from the bed. Watching her take me, arching her back while I grip her ass and sink deeper with every stroke, is the hottest thing I've ever seen.

"Oh shit," she groans.

"You like how fucking deep I am, love?"

"Yes, more."

"More," I agree, thrusting in until my balls slap up against her, and she's grabbing fistfuls of sheets while I indulge in one of my favorite fantasies and fuck her from behind.

Every day, her fans worship her.

Every night, I do.

When I let my hand drift up between her legs to circle her clit, she explodes, clenching on my cock so hard I come with a jolt. I grind against her, turning her chin to catch her moan of completion in a deep kiss as I follow her over.

The second time I take her, she's on top and we're face-to-face. Her nails rake my back, and I'm lost.

Turns out having someone brand you is fucking perfect, if it's the right someone.

I want this forever. Me, planning the next stage of my business—one that's no longer tethered to the past, but free to expand in the future. Her, triumphing in the club or working on a track. After, both of us coming together like this.

"I love you," I say after, pulling her toward me.

She traces the outline of my face, my jaw. "I love you too."

We lie across the satiny sheets, the glow from the headboard the only light in the bedroom. Behind the blackout curtains, the city throbs with its own nighttime energy.

"But...?" I prompt.

She's wearing that look, the one that says she's thinking hard about something.

"Tonight, you started to call me your girlfriend but didn't."

I can't stop the chuckle. "That's what you're worried about?"

"Not worried. Curious."

I stare her down until she starts to shift away, but I drag her back and tilt her chin up to me.

"I like you curious," I murmur against her neck.

"Go to sleep," she retorts, but she's smiling.

"And leave you awake to spin in that beautiful head of yours? Never."

One thing that hasn't changed is that it takes her awhile to wind down after a gig.

I brush my fingers through her hair.

"Not spinning. Thinking about your birthday next weekend," she says. "I have plans."

"You can't because I have plans."

"That's not how birthdays work." But her protest is softer, her breaths longer and slower.

I stroke down her arm and thread my fingers through hers, rubbing my thumb across each of her bare knuckles and memorizing the feel.

"It is now. I've been working on something too," I murmur.

But she's already asleep.

I smile.

EPILOGUE TWO

RAE

"You're joking," I blurt.

"I'm quite serious."

My hair blows around my face, and I brush it away to look around the deck of the yacht. "You *wanted* a boat for your birthday? Why the hell?"

Harrison follows my gaze, the wind tugging at his half-unbuttoned shirt. "Fond memories," is all he says, his mouth twitching in a cryptic smile as he takes my hand.

"You guys going to come and get drinks or what?" Beck calls.

Because, yeah, our friends came too. With Tyler

and Annie, a one-year-old Rose, Elle and Beck, it feels more like my birthday than Harrison's.

When Ash showed up, I knew this was a big deal. He flew over from the UK for only a couple of nights, arriving at the port thirty minutes after the rest of us given traffic from LAX.

Interestingly, Beck gave Ash more than his share of shit—probably because Ash did the same to Beck on my birthday when he'd been late. But as soon as they started sparring, it was impossible to stop them.

Something's up. I only found out we were going on an overnight trip when Harrison told me to pack a bag and then drove us to the port at Long Beach this morning.

I don't have a chance to press him as we set out to Catalina for the day, exploring the island together on bikes and on foot.

Harrison doesn't seem to be feeling any ill effects from the yacht—or maybe he's okay because we've spent more time on land than at sea.

After exploring Avalon and the Catalina Casino, we come back to the anchored yacht for a delicious chef-prepared dinner of swordfish, followed by cake.

"How fucking old do you think I am?" Harrison demands, taking in the dozens of candles interspersed with real flowers on the beautiful white cake.

"Don't blame me," Ash retorts, lifting a brow. "They know when you were born."

Annie, Elle, and I crack up. Even Rose gurgles, half-asleep in Annie's arms.

"You think this innocent act is gonna work forever?" Beck's arm leans across the back of Elle's chair, but his smirk is focused on Harrison's brother.

Ash leans over the table. "Not an act, Hollywood. What you see is what you get."

"The baker didn't want us to put candles on it, but we insisted," Tyler says, bringing the attention back to the cake.

Harrison shakes his head at me. But he's grinning.

I shift my chair closer to his.

"Wait. You have to make a wish, remember?" I prompt before he can blow out the candles. "And it'll only come true if you get them all in one breath."

He cocks his head. "You never told me what yours was."

I feel the flush crawling up my cheeks. "Maybe someday I will."

"In that case, I'll tell you mine when you tell me yours."

He blows, and every tiny flame extinguishes.

I wake up to a gentle rocking motion.

It takes a moment to recognize the stateroom in the dark.

The bed next to me is empty, and I frown. It can't be that long since we came down here.

After long looks over cake and drinks, we didn't even make it to the bed before Harrison lifted me up against the door and pressed inside me, his scent making my head spin while his hot breath fanned my throat.

But when we lay down together, me soaking in the perfection of this day, he seemed like the one locked in his head.

Now, sliding out from between the sheets, I tug on a shirt and shorts and head above deck, trying to be quiet so as not to wake Annie and Tyler or Rose or Elle or Beck.

At the top, the moonlight kisses the boat. The lights of Catalina are glittering jewels on the horizon.

Harrison leans over the railing, shirtless and in drawstring pants.

I take a moment to admire the view—of our surroundings, but equally, of him.

"Thinking of jumping off?" I tease, wrapping my arms around me against the breeze as I cross the deck to him.

He turns at the sound of my voice, chuckling. "Not seasick, love."

"Right." I lean over the railing next to him, staring down at the waves lapping against the yacht.

"Men like you charter yachts to fuck on them," I tease. Hard to believe it was more than a year and a half ago we had that conversation.

"It's not the only reason."

I sigh out a breath, relaxing into the evening.

He shifts off the railing, and it's only moments before I miss his company.

"Where did you..."

When I turn back, my words dry up.

Harrison's not standing behind me.

He's on one knee.

My heart stops. "Um. What are you doing?"

I grip the hem of my shirt, twisting it nervously in my fist.

I want to look around to see if this is some joke, but can't tear my eyes from him.

"Making my birthday wish come true," he replies.

He pulls out a small box and lifts the lid.

The blue-diamond teardrop, surrounded with white diamonds, sparkles back at me.

"I lived by my own rules until I met you. You were impossible and stubborn and..."

My eyebrows rise further.

"And I never want to live a day without you by my side." The breeze ruffles his hair, his throat bobbing with emotion. "You're already my queen, Reagan. Be my wife."

Holy shit.

I never thought of myself as the kind of girl to be swept off her feet, but there's no deck. No earth. Nothing stable to hold on to, except the commitment in his eyes.

I reach for the ring, lifting it out of the case and turning it in my fingers. The blue diamond is the size of my fingertip. He knew it was huge when he bought it. He probably doesn't know it's the same color as his eyes when he's inside me.

The band is wide enough for an inscription on the inside.

Through everything.

My throat tightens.

"Not because I merely want to survive what life throws at us," he murmurs, noticing me reading. "Because every day with you is an experience I will never take for granted."

I press my lips together.

"I want you with me always," he finishes.

I never thought much about a ceremony, but the idea of marrying him feels so damn right.

He's still larger than life, but maybe I am too. And it's the quiet moments with him I love the most —the teasing, the appreciating where we've come from, what we've been through together. When he tugs me against him at night.

"Well?" he prompts, looking agitated.

I take a breath. "Yes."

His grin flashes in the dark before he rises, towering over me again in a heartbeat. I'm already overwhelmed before he slips the ring on my finger, the cool metal feeling strange against my skin.

He pulls my lips up to his and kisses me with so much devotion and love and happiness that I'm speechless when he pulls back.

A noise has me looking up.

"Did it work?" Annie's head sticks up from the stairs that go belowdecks.

My jaw drops. "You were in on this?"

She tries to look innocent and fails.

"The best birthday gift," Harrison calls, loud enough for her to hear.

"You didn't like the bookcase?" I protest lightly, and he winks at me.

"It was stunning"—I had the custom furniture made to display his books in our place at the Wynn —"but this is even more beautiful and rare. And while that was something I didn't know I needed, you are quite simply someone I cannot live without."

Damn.

Suddenly our friends pour out of the stairway, surrounding us with love and congratulations. Elle carries a tray of bubbling champagne flutes while Ash claps his brother on the back and messes up my hair with a grin.

My heart is so full I can barely breathe.

"How are you guys going to do this?" Beck demands.

"Huge wedding," Harrison murmurs, wrapping an arm around me.

"Hell no," I retort, even as I rub my thumb over the inside of my ring to get used to the feel of it.

"We'll sell rights to *People* magazine," Beck promises.

"I'll sell your balls to them first." My eyes narrow. "If this is all some trick to get me to agree to honor and obey you—"

"I don't need that."

"Because I love you?"

He strokes a thumb along my jaw, reverent and possessive.

"That. And I still have a favor."

Thank you for reading BEAUTIFUL RUIN!

I hope you loved Harrison and Rae's story. Their honesty, rawness, and vulnerability got to me in a big way.

If you want more adventures in this world...they're coming! Sign up for my newsletter to get the latest details:

But first!

What happens when a man with everything loses it overnight?

Sawyer Redmond, who made a cameo in this book as Harrison's friend, is the hero in a new series coming this fall. It's hot, forbidden deliciousness. Order now to devour it release day!

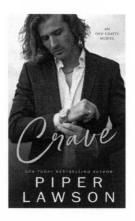

ONE CLICK CRAVE NOW >

If you enjoyed Beautiful Ruin, would you please consider leaving a quick review wherever you bought the book? Reviews are one of the best ways to support your favorite authors, and I'm grateful for each one!

Turn the page to read an exclusive preview of my hot new forbidden college romance CRAVE...

CHAPTER 1

OLIVIA

Gravel scrapes the soles of my Louboutins as I trip across the parking lot in the dark.

"The shoes are fucking hot," Kat says.

"They're not rated for off-roading," I reply.

She laughs and I send up a silent prayer for forgiveness as I dodge the empty beer cans.

Bad decisions have a slippery way of compounding. It's like when you drink one too many coffees in the morning, and next thing, you're headlining a cabaret with jazz hands.

The sign on the single-floor building in the middle of nowhere says "Velvet" in pink neon. The glow lingers in the corner of my vision when my friends line up at the bouncer, whose eyes have been on us since I was halfway across the lot.

He glances at Kat's ID, then Jules', but frowns at mine. "I don't think so, sweetheart." The license is fake, but before I can protest, he goes on. "You're drunk."

His gaze drops to my boobs, and the compassion I had for the guy doing his job melts away.

"I haven't had anything harder than soda tonight. You try walking across gravel in these."

"Yeah, I don't think so."

We're here for Kat, and as much as this isn't a place I'd choose to spend my night, it's not about me. It's about friendship.

"I'm better behaved than anyone in there," I insist. "Designated driver. Not my fault these shoes were designed with smooth surfaces in mind."

He stares at me like I'm nuts and I huff out a breath. "Fine. Would a drunk person be able to do this?"

I grab my shoe and bend my knee, pulling my foot up to the apex of my thighs. Then I take a breath before lifting it higher, straightening my leg so it's extended alongside my upper body.

His eyes round. I'm sure he's snuck a peek or two at the strippers who work the stage, but I've got moves he's never seen.

Releasing my leg, I grab my ID out of his hands and follow my friends.

"That was badass. I can't believe you did this for me!" Kat shouts over the music as we head inside.

"Tonight's about celebrating your birthday and

living life like a normal"—a glance back at the bouncer—"twenty-one-year-old."

I reach into my bag to pull out the Queen B tiara, and my roommate's eyes light up.

Kat's been bugging us for the past year to visit a part of town that's the opposite of the one starring in the glossy university recruitment brochures.

My corporate father and socialite mother would lose their shit if they saw me in a place like this.

Kat tugs us toward the bar since the booths around the perimeter are full. We wedge in, Jules calling for vodka sodas for her and Kat, and a Diet Coke for me.

On stage is a woman who looks too beautiful for this place. She winds around the pole, shifting toward the edge of the stage to drop her hips into a seductive slide.

When the dancer finishes, a woman dressed in a black T-shirt with the Velvet logo claims the mic.

"Shh, this is it," Kat breathes.

"This is what?" I demand.

"Amateur night!"

"You're not going up," Jules says, aghast.

Kat grins. "The prize is five hundred bucks. That's a helluva birthday present."

She brushes off her hands and joins the throng of girls by the register, returning a few minutes later with a white "Hello my name is" sticker that says "Cherry" stuck to her low-cut black tank.

"Subtle," I deadpan.

She hooks an arm around each of our necks, her long fingernails trailing across my bare shoulder.

I roll my eyes but end up doing a double take.

Down at the other end of the bar is a man who's so beautiful I nearly swallow my straw. His navy dress shirt is rolled to the elbows and tugs over rounded shoulders as he reaches for his drink. Dark hair past his jaw. Strong nose. Firm mouth. Eyes that scan the room, stopping when they meet mine.

It's electric, the connection. I swear he looks into me, through me. Fire grabs my core, making my breasts tighten and my thighs clench as I flush down to my toes.

"Liv. You okay?" Jules asks.

I blink, ripping my gaze from his to turn back to my friends. "Yeah."

I shake off the unsettling attraction.

He's the opposite of my boyfriend, Adam, who's blond and athletic with an easy smile. He's from the right family, has the right hair, and is the reserve point guard on the basketball team.

What I didn't tell Kat or Jules to avoid spoiling the birthday vibes is that when I showed up at his house yesterday morning, a girl was slipping out of his room.

Something in my chest popped like the cork on bad champagne.

I told myself if I dated Adam, at least one part of

my life would go as planned. After twelve years of wasted ballet, I couldn't be a dancer like my mother, but I had him.

"No fucking way."

Kat's pointing at a booth in the back, where a couple of guys from the basketball team sit, plus one I don't want to recognize.

Adam is sprawled across the bench with a half-naked woman bent over him, her boobs swinging dangerously close to his face.

My throat tightens as I wait for him to push her away.

Instead, he shifts back, grinning, and invites her closer.

"Unbelievable," Kat bites out. "I'm going to fuck him up."

Jules squeezes my shoulder, and I shake her off.

"Don't, Kat. It's probably some basketball team thing."

I turn toward the front, ignoring the back of the room and the burning behind my eyes.

We've invested three years. We'll figure this out. Maybe he screwed up, but he loves me.

I wonder if love feels the same for him as it does for me. If it's that dull reassurance I dig my fingers into when I'm feeling lost or if it's something else entirely.

The MC calls the contestants to the stage to explain the rules. "Each contestant has two minutes to dance, then the crowd will vote. First up is Brandy."

The first girl stands up as they play "Pour Some Sugar on Me."

She gyrates her hips, swinging around the pole, clearly drunk.

The next is a little better but not much.

At one point, a woman in the crowd yells, "Camera!" and security descends on a guy filming from inside his jacket with a phone to drag him out of the club.

It's comforting to know they enforce the "no videotaping" rule. The idea of dancing here on a dare and a few shots of vodka coming back to haunt you in perpetuity thanks to the internet is horrifying.

"Cherry!" the MC calls after a few minutes.

"That's you, Kat," Jules says, jarring me out of my numbness.

She gets up from the bar but trips. "Whoa. I can't, guys."

"You didn't pre-game that hard," Jules points out.

But Kat holds up a flask inside her bag I haven't seen before.

Shit.

Jules motions to the bartender for a water, but movement catches my eye. In the back, the woman dancing on Adam takes his hand, and he follows her with a shit-eating grin toward a doorway with a beaded curtain.

Bile rises up my throat.

My mom said not to give it up too fast or too slow. I slept with Adam three months into my senior year of high school, after his parents' party for winter break.

He said he liked that I made him wait.

Apparently, he likes that this woman won't.

I pull out my phone and type out a text.

Liv: I can't do this anymore, Adam. I think we should break up.

A moment after I hit send, he glances at his phone, shakes his head as if he's the one who can't believe *me*, and follows the woman through the curtain.

My chest squeezes hard. The walls I reinforced after catching him with that blonde this weekend crack, then crumble.

I told myself I'd let him off the hook if he convinced me it was a one-time thing.

But it's not. That callous dismissal of my text burns more than the jealousy. I've always tried to be the daughter my parents want, the girlfriend Adam needs, and none of it matters.

"'I Love Rock and Roll,'" starts up, its catchy hook emanating from the speakers.

The MC shouts for Cherry one more time.

"Liv?" Kat's peeling off the sticker and holding it out, her eyes imploring. "Do it for me?"

I'm not the girl who takes her clothes off when she's angry.

My parents raised me to see that women get ahead in this world through strategic social maneuvers, not brute force. I'm the girl who makes the other person feel comfortable, especially if they're the one who screwed up.

But the crowd's sneering faces blur together until they could be the girl who took Adam through that doorway. They could be my mom, who listened unmoved when I told her what I saw when I showed up at Adam's this weekend.

That cork in my chest is back in place, the contents of the bottle under more pressure than before.

I take the sticker and press it to my sleeveless white D&G tank top tucked into denim shorts.

When I start through the crowd, there's a wave of cheers. Each step is more confident than the last.

On stage, the bright lights are familiar, even if the audience of drunk and leering townies isn't.

The last time I danced for a crowd was years ago. Before...everything.

Nerves creep in until I catch the eye of the beautiful guy at the bar.

He's not leering. He's watching as if I'm the only person in this bar worth looking at.

The awareness is back, a tingling that cuts through my numbness. I'm borrowing from the conviction in his eyes, the expression that says he can't wait to see what I'll do next.

I stop in front of the pole, then reach back to wrap my hand around it. My back arches, my hair grazing my ass, and cheers go up.

I have what Kat calls "a great rack."

I call it "destroyer of dreams," "twin furies," "the unstoppables." When I turned sixteen, my boobs came in, and my ballet instructors sighed and crossed my name off their lists.

Tonight, no judgmental ballerinas are watching, and no beer bottles trip me up.

I lift my leg behind me in an arabesque. My fingers grab my stiletto, and I tug it toward the back of my head.

The more the crowd cheers, the deeper I go into the music. Into my own head.

The rhythm is low in my gut, and my feet move without instructions.

The tension feels raw and real and true.

I catch his eye again. His nostrils are flared, his jaw tight. For an instant, I pretend he sees me unlike everyone else in my life.

I pop my feet wide and sink into the splits.

It's not until I start to roll out of the pose that the sticky floor registers.

I'm barely up to standing when the woman in

the uniform is over to me, grabbing my hand and lifting it high.

"Our winner!" She passes me a check. "We have a tradition. You know what it is."

I don't notice the buckets at the side of the stage until two women dump them over me.

The shock of cold drowns me in a wave that steals my breath.

It's not water. It's vodka.

I'm soaked from my shoulders to my toes. My nipples are hard points through my shirt. The only thing still dry is the check in my fingers, its amount less than the price of my alcohol-drowned outfit.

The shock eats into my power trip from being on stage as I stumble down the steps.

"That was epic, Liv!" Kat bellows when I reach them.

Jules bites her lip. "Are you okay?"

"Totally." My arms fold over my chest and the wet fabric sticking to my skin makes me cringe. "I'm going to the car for a sweater. Happy birthday. *Cherry*."

I pass the check to Kat with a wink. She tries to give it back, but I refuse, pushing through the crowd to the exit.

My white Audi is conspicuous in this parking lot. Most of the rest of the cars are more like the Dodge pickup between my car and the club, though there's a beautiful black Mercedes on my opposite side.

I glance back at the club as I fish the keys from my bag.

That's when a group of guys emerges from the door. Adam's one of them, and another guy pulls out a vape pen as they laugh.

"How was it?" one of the other guys asks.

Plink.

I sink to my knees to follow the keys I've dropped in the gravel, missing Adam's response.

It's dark, and I fumble around under the edge of the car. My eyes burn, a tear escaping down my cheek.

The crunch of gravel behind me makes me freeze. "This the after-party?"

I swipe at my face because crying in front of other people is a sign of weakness.

When I turn, my heart stops.

It's the guy from the bar. The beautiful one who watched me.

Up close, I'd peg him at late twenties, maybe thirty. He's tall and broad, dark hair grazing his jaw until he shoves it back impatiently.

"I'm not here to perv on you. I'm heading out." He glances at the pickup truck. "Wanted to make sure you weren't driving drunk."

"I'm getting a change of clothes."

His gaze drops to my chest. My nipples are still sticking through the shirt. "Good call."

He starts toward the hood, probably to round to the driver's side of his truck, but I grab his sleeve.

"Don't leave. That's my boyfriend. Ex-boyfriend," I amend, the word I've never used before echoing in my ears. "If you move your truck, he'll see my car."

The gorgeous man looks between the Dodge and the Audi.

"Just...wait until they finish their vape?" I plead.

He doesn't respond but doesn't move either.

I unlock the car and lean into the back seat, rummaging for my sweatshirt. My fingers sink into the soft fabric of the hoodie.

"What are you doing here?" I ask over my shoulder.

"Came to town for some unfinished business."

I sneak a look. He's facing the other way to either give me privacy or stand watch.

I tug the sticky shirt over my head, wadding it into a ball and dropping it on the back seat with a grimace.

"I meant at a strip club. You don't look like the type to ogle tits and drown your sorrows."

The low rumble of laughter behind me makes my skin tingle. "You don't look like the type to shake your tits to forget your problems."

I pull on the sweatshirt and shift back out of the car, the hood still up around my head. "So what's your excuse?"

I catch sight of my reflection—smudged makeup,

tangled hair—in the passenger mirror. But the man turns back to me before I can even think of trying to fix it, his gaze finding mine unerringly in the dark. "I hate doing what people expect."

A rush of adrenaline races through me. "So you didn't ogle my tits?" It's not like me to tease a stranger. Blame it on the vodka fumes.

"I'm a man who appreciates beautiful things."

The heat in his eyes steals my breath. It's sexual, but more than that, it's like he's talking about watching fireworks or a once-in-a-lifetime meteor shower.

He does a double take at the logo on my chest. "Russell U. You're an alum, too?"

Before I can respond, riotous laughter goes up from across the lot.

"Fucking A, Adam!"

"Ignore him," he murmurs. I blink up at the man in front of me, who tugs the hood off my head. "Why'd you want me to watch you dance?"

My brows shoot up. "What makes you think I did?"

"You wanted everyone to, or you wouldn't have been up there. A woman like you is desired. I think you're tired of the reason people desire you."

There's no reason I should be smiling tonight, but the way this man looks at me, like my life isn't over, has me gulping night air.

"I'm Sawyer." He bends to pick up something

from the ground. The sticker from my shirt. "Nice to meet you, Cherry."

"Come on, let's get out of here." A voice carries on the breeze.

Adam and the other guys cut across the lot, and my heart rises up my throat as I scan the lot and notice the RU Basketball bumper sticker on the Jeep in the next row.

If they don't notice my car, they'll still notice me when they head this way.

I duck behind Sawyer. "Quick. Act like you're my boyfriend."

A brow lifts. "You want me to pick a fight with you?"

My eyes roll hard. "That's what you think of? No, just—" I grab his jacket collar and drag him down to the ground with me.

I land hard enough the gravel scrapes my knee.

We're crouched between the cars. He's inches away, and my heart skips because of how he's looking at me. Not me on stage. Me in my hoodie, makeup smudged.

His expression says he doesn't give a fuck.

I never realized how badly I've been longing for someone to look at me this way.

"You didn't want me to argue with you," he murmurs, a mocking lilt to his voice. "You wanted me to kiss you."

I'm not sure I was thinking at all when I said it.

But heat strokes down my spine at the thought of his mouth on mine.

I swallow hard. "You make it sound so sexy."

"It is sexy." His throat flexes, and the way he says that word is the hottest thing I've ever heard. "A kiss is a promise. A declaration of intent."

"Most guys think anything less than a blowjob doesn't deserve their attention."

Sawyer shifts closer, his gaze knowing. His fingers find my hair, tucking it behind my ear and leaving my skin tingling.

His lips are an inch from mine. I've never felt this kind of chemistry with anyone, and he's practically a stranger.

"Do me a favor, Cherry. Don't judge me by that tool."

Before I can respond, he leans in and brushes his mouth over mine.

It's gentle, with so much fucking finesse. His lips are firm, sweeping across the curve of mine.

When he changes the angle, taking me deeper, I can't help but open under him.

The gravel is rough on my bare knees, but his kiss is exquisite. He's exquisite.

A soft sound escapes, a moan, but it's lost in his mouth. I should be embarrassed, but there's no room for it.

His fingers find my chin, holding me in place. Where the hell would I go?

When he pulls back, it's all I can do not to say wow.

His breathing is rough, too, those gorgeous eyes dilated in the dark.

"You taste like trouble," he murmurs.

A thrill races through me because I'm sure no one has ever described me like that before.

"I'm going to give you my number," he goes on.

My chest tightens with shock. "You're asking me out?"

The surprise on his face is chased by a grin. "Tonight, you're going to let me know you got home safely."

And what about tomorrow? I want to ask.

But as he takes my phone and types in his contact, I'm relieved. Adam cheated on me, and I'll break up with him in person tomorrow...but this is moving fast.

I tuck my phone back into my purse and straighten to test whether my knees still work.

Barely.

I survey the parking lot. "They're gone."

He's up the next second too, tall enough his jaw is eye level on me. He checks his watch. "You have to work early too?"

Of course he thinks I'm older. Students don't come here.

I can't tell him I'm a college junior, that tomorrow is the first day of classes in my third year, not when he's clearly got life figured out. If adulting is an art, this man is Rembrandt.

"Let me guess. You'd rather take a bullet," he says before I can respond. "I know the feeling."

His gaze fixes on my legs, and he bends to brush his fingers across my knee, loosening the bits of gravel stuck to it.

What could a man like him dread? He's gorgeous, confident, charismatic in a doesn't-have-to-try way.

His thumb brushes my cheek, grazing the diamond stud in my ear. "I hope tomorrow's better than you expect. Don't let anyone drag you down, Cherry."

As he rounds my hood, he heads for the Mercedes on the far side.

The truck isn't his.

When he peels out of the lot, disappearing in a glimmer of red taillights and New York plates, I'm left to wonder why the hell a man like that helped a girl like me.

But the next breath I take is cold night air and engine fumes, and I swear nothing ever tasted so good.

ONE CLICK CRAVE NOW >

BOOKS BY PIPER LAWSON

ENEMIES SERIES

Beautiful Enemy

Beautiful Sins

Beautiful Ruin

RIVALS SERIES

Love Notes

A Love Song for Liars

A Love Song for Rebels

A Love Song for Dreamers

A Love Song for Always

WICKED SERIES

Good Girl

Bad Girl

Wicked Girl

Forever Wicked

Wicked 1-3 Box Set

MODERN ROMANCE SERIES

Easy Love

Bad Love

THANK YOU

My readers are the most amazing readers anywhere. You guys are positive, bold, enthusiastic, supportive, and you inspire me daily.

If you enjoyed *Beautiful Ruin*, I'd be beyond grateful if you could take two minutes to leave a quick review wherever you picked it up. Reviews are like gold to us authors.

If you do leave a review, I'd love to hear about it so I can thank you personally. Here're the best ways to reach out:
www.facebook.com/piperlawsonbooks
www.instagram.com/piperlawsonbooks
piper@piperlawsonbooks.com

Make sure you're on my VIP list to get updates, special giveaways and deals! Signup at: https://www.piperlawsonbooks.com/subscribe

Thanks for being awesome, for inspiring me, and for helping make it possible for me to do what I love.

xo,

Piper

ACKNOWLEDGMENTS

Harrison and Rae have been in my head in various forms for almost two years now. Back when I was writing Tyler and Annie, these two kept tugging at my heart.

This story wouldn't have happened without the support of my awesome readers, including my ARC team. You ladies provide endless enthusiasm, cheer-leading, and help spreading the word. I could NOT do it without you, and it would be a lot less fun to try.

An extra shoutout to Tal, Suzanne, Anna and Tina for reading early! You guys are awesome and your input was so on point.

Thank you Regina Wamba for the perfect image.

This couple has been inspiring me for more than a year.

Becca Mysoor, thank you for your story genius. Cassie Robertson and Devon Burke, thank you for questioning, polishing, and catching all the little things.

Thank you Dani Sanchez for your sage advice and for helping my stories find their way to the right readers.

And Annette Brignac and Michelle Clay... I would not be able to get these books to the people who matter most without you. Don't ever leave me.

Thank you all from the bottom of my heart. The best part of author life is having YOU in it.

Love always,

Piper

ABOUT THE AUTHOR

Piper Lawson is a Wall Street Journal and USA Today bestselling author of smart, steamy romance! She writes about women who follow their dreams (even the scary ones), best friends who know your dirty secrets (and love you anyway), and complex heroes you'll fall hard for (especially after talking with them). Brains or brawn? She'll never make you choose.

Piper lives in Canada with her tall, dark and brilliant husband. She believes peanut butter is a protein, rose gold is a neutral, and love is ALWAYS the answer.

I love hearing from you! Hang with me on:

The Interwebs➜www.piperlawsonbooks.com
Facebook➜www.facebook.com/piperlawsonbooks
Newsletter➜www.piperlawsonbooks.com/subscribe
Instagram➜www.instagram.com/piperlawsonbooks
Goodreads➜www.goodreads.com/author/
show/13680088

Made in the USA
Middletown, DE
28 November 2021